Growing Young

A Simple Love Story: Book 2

Dana LeCheminant

Cover design copyright © 2019 by Sheridan Bronson
Cover image © 2019 by MJTH/Shutterstock.com
Graphic element © Vecteezy.com

First Printing: December 2019

ISBN: 978-1-951753-01-6

To those willing to take a chance:
I promise happier endings from here on out

CHAPTER ONE

December 2014

"Good afternoon, passengers. We will be landing in about ten minutes. Please return your seats to their upright positions and put up your tray tables while the flight attendants make their final checks. The weather in Sacramento is a lovely fifty degrees, and local time is 2:37 p.m."

The voice overhead might as well have been condemning me to a month of agonizing torture. It was as if the pilot knew I was headed for my worst nightmare, and she wanted nothing more than to be absolutely cheerful and optimistic in light of my very real troubles. If I could just get up there and tell her exactly what I thought of her overly friendly voice, maybe she'd turn the plane around and head back to Maryland. I already had to get up ungodly early to make my flight and hadn't managed to ditch the driver Dad sent to make sure I actually got on the plane. It wasn't like sleeping on planes or trying to dodge chaperones was an easy feat, so I was exhausted.

"Is there anything I can get you before we land, Miss Davenport?"

I shoved my sleeping mask from my eyes to stare up at the flight attendant who had done his very best to make the entire flight miserable. I was sure he saw his friendliness as endearing, even helpful, but after he refused to bring me a good, stiff drink—"I'm sorry, Miss Davenport, but you're only seventeen. Would you like a soda?"—I decided he wasn't worth paying attention to. Yes, I was only seventeen, but that hadn't stopped a good many flight attendants from slipping me at the very least champagne. Most of the time it only took me a smile to get exactly what I wanted.

The awful man still stood there by my bed, all smiles and politeness that made me want to gag because none of it was real.

"Xanax?" I tried, though I could guess his response.

"Ginger ale?" he replied. His name tag said Hamir. I could only guess how he managed to sound so American.

With an exaggerated sigh, I shoved my many blankets off of me and struggled to sit up. "Don't you have some business class person to annoy?" I grumbled.

Somehow, his smile didn't even falter. Either he'd been doing this job for a long time, or that grin was permanently plastered to his face. "Your father was very specific in his instructions that you be well looked after, Miss Davenport." Which meant dear Hamir had been paid handsomely for the five-and-a-half-hour flight.

Oh, my father. Always trying to hide the fact he was not really a father at all. Luckily I turned out just fine despite his negligence, but he seemed to think I had no idea he was crap at the whole parenting thing simply because his money followed me wherever I went. Not that I complained about that part.

"Get this plane to go to the Bahamas," I told Hamir bitterly. "That's where I'm supposed to be at Christmas. Not stupid California." But no. Dad decided he and his new wife needed to go to Prague on their honeymoon and sent me off to whichever relative he could pay to babysit me. I should have been basking on warm, sunny beaches like I always did for Christmas, but while Dad got a vacation without me, I was left to scowl at the plainness of the Sacramento landscape as we descended.

I'd never been to Prague.

"That's unfortunately out of my power, Miss Davenport," Hamir replied, ever smiling and ever present. Better than I could say for my family. "I hear Lake Tahoe is beautiful at Christmas."

I had a good number of things I wanted to say to Hamir, but I held my tongue, only because I figured the woman sitting across the aisle from me would throw up yet again if she heard me. I had no desire to add my more colorful language capabilities to her motion sickness.

And though I gave him my best scowl, Hamir just smiled and indicated I should put on my seatbelt before he went off to check on the other first-class passengers. So that was that. The one person who was supposed to take care of me had abandoned me to my old cousin and her husband who was probably a good twenty years older than her, as they tended to be. In my world, women went where the money was, no matter how old the man who had it.

Lanna Davenport. I hadn't seen my cousin Lanna since I was a kid, and Dad expected me to be happy about going to stay with her? She was ten years older than me, and the last time I'd seen her, she was the most depressing person I'd ever met. She never wanted to play with dolls, and she never went shopping with us, and she was always knocking things over and tripping on her own feet. Dad said he wasn't sure how she could be a Davenport, that she had too much of her mom in her, and he always talked about her like she was going to be a disgrace to the family name. The whole family was a waste, he said. One son went and got himself killed in a car accident, and the other drank himself into embarrassment.

I was as shocked as he was when we got a wedding invitation in the mail a few months ago, telling us she was marrying into one of the more famous families in Northern California. How her mom had managed to pull that one off, neither of us knew. Her husband, Dad said, was a Munroe, which meant he ran one of the biggest art trade companies in the country. Part of me wanted to go to the wedding, just to see how ugly the man was if he settled for someone as pathetic as Lanna.

But I had my standards.

And yet now I was stuck on a plane in the middle of December, about to spend about a month with the worst relatives, and there was nothing I could do about it unless I managed to avoid them after the plane landed. One more week, and I could have been left on my own. I was only a week away from legal adulthood, but Dad refused to accept my reasoning that I could survive a single week until that magical moment my age changed and I could do what I wanted. I suspected his new bride Daruska had something to do with that decision. Until he hitched himself to her Czechoslovakian wagon, he'd never had a problem with me taking a trip to Paris or Cabo on my own.

"Miss Davenport, welcome to Sacramento."

I shuddered as I followed Hamir off the plane. *Sacramento.* It couldn't have been Long Beach or even San Francisco? No, dear cousin Lanna had to think a place as lowbrow as Lake Tahoe was a fine place for a vacation. It was like she was raised in a stable. To think,

I could have been in my favorite bikini by now, flirting with a cabana boy. But no, I was heading for the worst month of my life.

Unless I took matters into my own hands… As soon as I got my luggage, I had an entire airport at my fingertips, and if I played my cards right, I could be on a flight to Venice before anyone realized I hadn't shown up yet.

"Catherine?" a deep voice said before I'd even fully cleared the gate yet.

You've got to be kidding me. Dad must have really worked hard to make sure I didn't run off, and in a strange way it almost made me think he cared. But that was ridiculous. He didn't care about me arriving to my family safely; he cared about me embarrassing him while he was enjoying his actual vacation.

But when I looked up and locked eyes with the guy who had spoken my name, I found myself smiling just a bit. He was gorgeous, tall and solid and with a sharp jaw as his blue eyes took me in. "Catherine, right?" he repeated. "Lanna's waiting in the main terminal."

Had she sent a driver to fetch me? Probably. And I flashed him the smile that had gotten me a car for my sixteenth birthday from a man I didn't even know, because if this guy was going to be hanging around the next month, maybe it wouldn't be all that bad. "That's me," I said sweetly.

He held out a large hand for me to shake. "Adam," he said. "Shall we?" He headed for the baggage claim where my trolley would be waiting for me, and I slipped my arm through his before we made it very far. He gave me a look from the corner of his eye, and I smiled up at him, making his ears turn red. Goodness, he was tall. And smelled incredible, like Florida oranges. And though he put his hands in his pockets and hunched over a bit so he didn't stand out quite so much, the shyness didn't dissuade me from making a plan to charm him completely before we even hit the car. I could probably persuade him to drive me away from my fate if I had enough time to wear him down.

"Over here, Adam," a woman said, and instantly I prickled. I usually didn't mind a bit of competition, but I was too tired to fight for the affection of the handsome driver right now.

Adam perked up, standing straighter as a grin lit up his face. He slipped out of my hold and picked up his pace, heading straight for the pretty blonde who waved at him. Without so much as a word of greeting, he slipped his arms around her waist and held her like no one was watching, even though everyone in the area was.

Huffing, I grit my teeth and grumbled as I got buffeted by the crowd. It was the perfect time to try to make a run for it, but I couldn't help but glare at the woman who had already claimed my best chance at escape. She was about my same height, similar in size as well, but she had the most incredible golden hair, long and wavy and perfect. I'd always wanted to be blonde, but I'd gotten stuck with boring brown. I'd tried to go blonde once, but it hadn't gone well. Mom had given me too olive a skin tone to pull it off.

"Catherine?" the woman asked, having finally gotten her fill of the handsome man.

I stared at her, trying to figure out why she was looking at me with awe. I mean, I didn't blame her, and it wasn't like she was the only one in the vicinity who couldn't keep her eyes off me as I stood there. But there was something familiar about her, something in the way her nose crinkled when she smiled. It reminded me a bit of Dad.

"Lanna?" I gasped.

She broke into a grin, grabbing Adam's hand and moving closer. "Good glory, Catherine, you've grown up so much! I was half expecting you to still be in kindergarten."

How did awkward Lanna turn into Malibu Barbie? Well, Barbie in jeans and a t-shirt, but still. Put her in a dress, and she would have fit right in with the parties I went to. But if this was Lanna… I turned to Adam and felt my face flush with heat as I realized who he had to be.

"You've already met my husband," Lanna said, catching my gaze.

Handsome hunk of meat was married to *Lanna*? I was suddenly glad I hadn't tried any harder to seduce him into taking me somewhere.

"And where did Matthew go?" she continued, unaware of how Adam seemed to hunch even smaller, which meant he'd probably noticed my attempts, even if they were small.

"Right here," someone new answered, his voice a little breathless. He came from the side, my luggage trolley in front of him and a ridiculous grin as he met my eye. "Jeez, Kitty, did you bring your whole closet with you?"

Matthew. I had a cousin named Matthew. Clearly he wasn't the one who died, but he didn't look like a hopeless drunk either. Especially when his eyes darted about, taking in the people around us in the keen way only someone who was trained to be alert and observant could. But he used my childhood nickname I hated so much, so he couldn't be anyone but Lanna's supposedly alcoholic brother. And I had a feeling he was going to make it much harder to get away from this place than I hoped.

I should have run when I still could.

"I think we've terrified her into silence," Lanna mock whispered to Adam.

"You do that to everyone," Matthew replied, leaning on the trolley and looking about ready to laugh as he took in whatever incredulous expression I had on my face. "So, Kitty, are you ready to see what West Coast Davenport life is like?"

Not a single one of them looked how they should. They were *elites*. High society. The best of the best. I should have recognized what they were just by the smell of their $1000 cologne and a wardrobe that screamed of wealth. But no. They just stood there in the middle of an airport looking completely…normal. Average. And I had a feeling their mediocrity didn't just exist in their fashion sense.

This was going to be the worst month of my life.

"What are we standing around for?" I grumbled. "Take me to my prison."

CHAPTER TWO

"Good morning, Catherine." Lanna greeted me down in the kitchen of their Tahoe shack looking like she'd crawled straight out of bed. Didn't she care that her hair was only half in her braid or that she looked tired without makeup on? Ugh, was that *pizza* printed on her pajama bottoms? "Do you want some breakfast?" She was drawing something in a notebook as she sat at the countertop, half a banana in her other hand.

I glanced at the loaf of bread sitting next to the toaster and did my best not to wrinkle my nose at it. My father may not have taught me much, but I knew not to be rude to family. Especially rich family, though I never would have guessed these people had any sort of funds looking at the place they chose to spend their Christmas. The house only had four bedrooms. *Two* bathrooms. I had to share a bathroom with my cousin Matthew, though Lanna had assured me upon arrival that he would only use up all the hot water every other day and give me the chance to do the same on the others.

"I'll pass," I muttered, settling in a chair that looked like it probably came from Sears.

It had been bad enough when I realized Dad had frozen my credit cards so I couldn't buy myself a ride, but everything about this place was like it was designed to make me miss my life even more than I already was.

Adam came into the kitchen a second later, first tossing a couple pieces of sliced grocery store bread into the toaster then giving his wife a kiss that nearly made her drop the banana to the floor. "How do you get more and more beautiful every time I see you?" he asked as if it were the most natural question in the world.

Lanna simply beamed as she watched him grab some peanut butter from a cupboard above the toaster.

"Sickening, aren't they?" Matthew asked behind me. He, at least, knew how to get ready in the morning. He may not have been wearing designer, but at least he wouldn't look completely out of place if he showed up at the club. The black t-shirt and dark jeans he wore suited him well. Pulling up the chair next to me, he sat on it backwards and rested his arms on the back as he watched his sister suddenly shriek and duck away from the man who decided he needed to shove his hand into the jar of peanut butter and try to smear it on Lanna's face.

I'd spent the entire two-hour drive listening to them whisper and giggle in the front seats of the car like they were little girls. Sickening was pretty close to the mark. "Uh, how long have they been together?" I asked, though I would have known if I'd actually wasted a trip coming to their wedding. Was I suddenly part of their honeymoon without wanting to be? *Just kill me now.*

Matthew chuckled, resting his chin on his arms. "Married more than a year," he said, "together almost two. Not that you'd ever guess it's been that long." Clearly I hadn't paid much attention to that wedding invitation if it had come that long ago.

"I've seen dating couples who haven't looked this happy," I observed, more to myself than anything. After my dad's third marriage, I decided happiness in marriage probably wasn't a real thing. Suddenly I doubted that opinion, especially when Adam touched a tender kiss to Lanna's forehead and sent her blushing like crazy. No one who saw the pair of them could think they were anything but blissfully in love.

"Hey!" Matthew said, loud enough to draw the Munroes' attention. "I'm heading into town. Need anything?"

"More peanut butter," Adam replied, which drew a very unflattering snort from Lanna.

"No," she said, fighting a laugh, "we're good. Catherine?"

Wait, were they asking if I had a *grocery list*? What I needed was to get as far from this place as I could.

"You're welcome to join me," Matthew added to me. "I know the pair of them can be overwhelming."

Anything to get out of feeling like I'd just entered another reality. "Get me out of here," I said and grabbed my phone.

As we walked to the car parked outside The Shack—aka the not-so-fancy Munroe vacation home—Matthew's eyes kept darting around at every little movement again. It would have made me nervous if I hadn't seen it before in the men Dad always hired whenever we went to the bigger cities. "What do you do for work, Matthew?" I asked. What was Uncle Harris's job again? A lawyer or a doctor or something. Like literally everyone else I knew.

Matthew laughed and surprisingly had the decency to open my door for me. Once he was in his own seat, he gave me a smile. "Sorry if I make you tense. Lanna says it drives her crazy, especially when we're out here, but it's hard to break out of the habit."

"You're a bodyguard?" I guessed.

He nodded, backing up then heading for the road. The Munroe house was quite a ways off from the others on the street, which only added to the suffocating feel of it. Even if I tried to escape, it wouldn't be easy to get anywhere that could pass as an improvement to my current situation. Five more days, and I would be eighteen. Five more days, and Dad couldn't force me to stay anywhere.

"I keep Adam and his dad safe, especially when they have their bigger galleries and exhibits on display. Their line of work can get…dangerous." His voice trailed off a little as a shadow passed his face. What was he thinking about? Not that I cared. "Anyway, they keep telling me I'm not here to work, but I can't help it. I see what I see, and I'll protect the people I care about. No matter what."

So Matthew would make escaping harder here too. I would have to keep that in mind as I made my plans.

Halfway into town, I had to stop looking, just because it felt like I'd passed into one of those charity neighborhoods you only drove through to make yourself feel better about the state of your life. People really considered this a vacation? On top of that, it was freezing, and I stared at the dirty snow that lined the roads, wondering why anyone would even bother to live here.

Instead of looking out the window, I pulled out my phone and started searching for what people even did in this town for fun. If Matthew really was a bodyguard, I had a feeling he wouldn't let me leave The Shack unless he was with me, and it would be easier to get away if there were other people around. I found a few bars, some restaurants. Nothing to help me escape before my birthday. Five more days at the most, then I could go somewhere with a pool and a chef who could make me a green smoothie instead of expecting me to eat the junk they called bread. I never thought I'd miss Paris for the carbs, but there I was.

"Do you ski?" Matthew asked, and he glanced at my phone screen as I went through a list of top attractions in the area.

Of course I skied. I wasn't raised like a savage. "I doubt these'll compare to the Alps," I replied dryly.

"You should give them a try anyway. I'm sure Adam would be happy to take you with him."

Ah, dear cousin Matthew. He had no idea how much I had no intention of befriending any of them. Although, if I went skiing with Adam, I could probably give him the slip then catch myself a ride out of the resort and at least into town so I could pay someone to take me back to the airport. Somehow.

"Maybe not skiing," Matthew muttered, giving me some impressive side eye.

I swallowed an insult, not because I didn't want to say it to him but because I knew if I estranged our family any further, Dad would find out about it. He may not have said it out loud, but I was pretty sure he wanted me to stay with family instead of a hired chaperone just for the sake of keeping things relatively close with his brother and his family. Should the need ever arise—though he assured me it wouldn't—we didn't want to be completely destitute. Keeping up relationships meant we would never be out on the streets.

"What are we doing here anyway?" I asked as Matthew pulled into the parking lot of what looked like a family-run supermarket. "Don't you have staff for this?"

"Not here," he replied as he came around to open my door. "I know it's not what you're used to, Catherine, but you'll get the hang of this eventually. Adam and Lanna like to get away from the craziness of our world when they can, and buying their own food and cleaning the house themselves helps them feel like they lead simple lives."

"Why would anyone want something simple?" I grumbled. Were their whole lives just out in the open for each other to see? That sounded horrible. Then I froze. "Cleaning?" I asked. "They do that themselves?" Oh great, would they expect me to join in? I didn't care what they threatened me with, because I was way too above sticking my hands inside a toilet.

Matthew laughed. "Cleaning. Cooking. Laundry. Out here, they're regular Jack and Jill."

Did the nightmare never end? I clutched my phone tighter. Unless I went insane over the next week, that phone was my only lifeline to the real world. I would do my very best to never part with it. Otherwise I wouldn't survive.

"Are you coming in with me or just hanging out in the car?" Matthew asked, and he narrowed his eyes a little as he waited for my answer. His finger rested on the lock button, and I had a feeling he would rather lock me in than let me go wandering around town looking for a way out. How did he even know what I was thinking?

"I guess I don't have a choice," I sighed and slid out of the car to follow him to the grungy store.

* * *

Lanna asked me every meal if I wanted to help. It was like she expected me to do my share of the work, and no matter how many times I rolled my eyes and ignored her, she kept asking. By the third day trapped in the house, even Adam had taken to making little comments about how I spent all my time in my tiny little bedroom glued to my phone, but what did they expect me to do? *They* chose to live like common middle class. *I* did not. I couldn't stop my dad from sending me to stay with them, but I wasn't about to let them make me feel less than the princess I was.

Matthew was the worst. He may not have asked me to help wash the dishes after dinner, but he somehow managed to know exactly where I was every second of every day. If I went downstairs to sneak out while Lanna and Adam were taking a nap, Matthew was there reading a book. If I stayed in my room, he was just across the hall watching TV but probably listening to make sure I didn't call in a rescue squad. If I snuck outside in the middle of the night, he was out making a snowman. Who even made snowmen unless they were eight? And at three in the morning, no less? And when he saw me standing there on the porch bundled in every coat I owned, he simply smiled and stuck a carrot into the snowman's face to give it a nose.

No matter where I went or what I did, my dear cousin's eyes were on me, and it was getting ridiculous.

Either Dad had specifically asked him to keep a close watch, knowing my tendency to do what I wanted, or Matthew Davenport could read minds and knew I was trying to find a way to escape. He was either a very good bodyguard or completely creepy. Probably both. And thanks to him, the days in The Shack dragged on.

"Come play a game with me, Catherine." Matthew stood in my doorway, leaning against the frame and smiling at me like he'd suggested something I would actually want to do.

I glanced down at my phone, where all my pleas for help went unanswered. Apparently all my friends had better things to do during Christmas break than help me figure out a way out of this hell. Didn't they realize they were my only hope? Victoria could send her helicopter to rescue me. Davis could come up from San Francisco in his Mercedes and whisk me off to the airport so we could head to London like we did a couple of years ago. But my phone hadn't beeped at me in days, so it was looking like I was going to have to save myself.

Big surprise there.

Tomorrow was my birthday, and after that I'd be free to do what I wanted. As long as I found a way out of The Shack.

"A game?" I moaned when Matthew didn't get the hint from my silence. "I don't play games."

Matthew actually laughed. *Infuriating.* It was like nothing bothered him at all, and I had to wonder how he could smile so easily all the time. "I have a feeling that's not entirely true," he said. "Come on. Lanna says you're good at poker. Come play a few hands, and you can steal my inheritance."

I almost smiled, but I wasn't about to let him think he could sometimes be amusing. But really, with his charm and his family name, he could be the center of attention in the wealthy world, and instead he just hung around the nauseating Munroe pair and hid in the background. He may have been a bodyguard, but he was still a Davenport. Wasted potential, if you asked me.

"Fine," I said finally. "But don't try to let me win."

"Wouldn't dream of it," he replied and led the way downstairs.

Adam and Lanna were just in the other room decorating the little Christmas tree they'd gone out and cut yesterday. As usual, they'd asked if I wanted to join them on their little excursion, but trudging through the cold and snow sounded worse than being stuck in The Shack. Now I almost wished I'd gone with them, just because I could have found a much better tree than the limp thing they chose. It practically sagged in its little stand and reminded me of that Peanuts tree that could barely hold its single ornament. *Pathetic.*

Lanna was adding each ornament with strange precision, choosing each position as if it were a life and death decision. Somehow Adam didn't mind the time it took before he could hand her another one, and he just sat there grinning at her like he'd never seen anything more fascinating. I couldn't help but stare as Adam took Lanna's hand and pulled her close so he could rest his head against her arm for just a moment, and Lanna closed her eyes as if she couldn't imagine being happier. How were those two even real?

"Want to join us, Catherine?" Lanna asked once she looked over and saw me standing by the table.

I raised an eyebrow. "We had a decorator who did that," I replied, though no one had bothered to put up decorations this year.

"It's really fun," she insisted.

I had no intention of messing up what she clearly thought was perfection. "I have to take all of Matthew's money," I said and settled at the table. I had no idea how she knew, but Lanna was right. I *was* good at poker. I'd once won ten thousand bucks in Vegas in a single game and would have kept playing if someone didn't recognize me and tell the casino I was only sixteen at the time.

As Matthew shuffled and dealt the cards, I kept watching my cousin. I had to admit, Lanna was surprising. Not at all what I expected, and her husband certainly wasn't as old as I'd pictured. I still had no idea how she'd managed to convince a specimen like that to even give her a second glance, but at least she didn't disgrace the family name by settling for some gardener or grocery store clerk or something. That would have been embarrassing, and it was nice to know that if Lanna Davenport could snag herself a rich and handsome catch, someone much better equipped shouldn't have a problem. I had no intention of settling down any time soon, but that wouldn't stop me from exploring my options. A lot.

"Catherine, we have a surprise for you," Lanna said halfway through our first hand. Somehow she'd ended up with half the tinsel all over her head, and I suspected Adam was behind it, seeing as he grinned like a dork behind her. Honestly, didn't they care what people thought?

"Oh goody," I replied sarcastically. "Are you going to let me put the star on top?"

Matthew chuckled, shaking his head, but Lanna wasn't discouraged. "You're welcome to if you want," she said, "but I have a feeling this is something more your speed." She looked at her husband, who nodded and cleared his throat.

I was pretty sure I hadn't heard the handsome Adam Munroe speak more than a sentence or two at a time, so I was curious to see what he might have to say. He wasn't exactly talkative, though he made up for it with his dazzling smile. "We have a new Klimt we're planning to display at a gala tomorrow before it goes to auction."

I stared at him. "I don't know what that is," I admitted, even though Lanna looked monumentally excited about the idea. Gala, on the other hand, I understood. "What sort of gala?" I asked.

"The fancy kind," Matthew said and wiggled his eyebrows. "One where you can wear the fanciest dress you want."

I still wasn't convinced. "Private?"

"Invitation only," Lanna confirmed. All three of them were looking at me warily, as if my response was the most important sentence of the day. Lanna had something to add, however: "I know it's your birthday tomorrow, and you don't have to go if you don't want to. But I know you've been bored, so maybe this will be a good way to make you feel a little more at home."

Not likely. Still, if they were busy talking to the nobodies who would show, I'd have a better chance of escaping.

"I'll be there too," Matthew said quietly. I could swear he could read my thoughts, and I narrowed my eyes at him and thought of some good words he would blush to hear out loud. But my cousin just winked at me and laid down a perfect hand of cards.

I took that as a sign I didn't really have a choice about this "fancy" party of theirs. "Fine," I said. "As long as I don't have to talk to any-one."

CHAPTER THREE

"Miss Davenport, you look every bit as beautiful as your cousin."

How did everyone know who I was? I'd spent almost an hour trapped in one place because people kept coming up to me, determined to say hi. Some even wished me a happy birthday, and I couldn't decide which of my cousins was to blame for that. Lanna seemed too busy hanging on Adam's arm to have time to tell anyone, and Matthew didn't seem to have spoken to anyone since we arrived. He just stood on the other side of the room and watched me unblinkingly. Even when I tried to focus on something or someone else, I could feel his eyes on me.

Definitely not a drunken mess.

"Good evening, Miss Davenport." The man who spoke bowed his head a little, and while his hair was peppered with gray, he was still pretty attractive compared to some of the losers I'd had to pretend to be friendly to. "I'm glad you were able to come to my gala."

I furrowed my brow as he placed a kiss on my hand. "Your gala?" I asked, though there was something else about him that was bothering me. I just couldn't place what it was. "I thought—"

"Adam Munroe is the face of the company, yes," he admitted, "but he leaves the event planning to me. Social interaction isn't exactly The Prince's forte."

I'd heard him called that before, 'The Prince of Art,' but I hadn't realized how well known my cousin-in-law actually was. People he'd never met, from what I could tell, went straight for him and tried to be his best friend. And the poor man probably would have crumbled from all the pressure of speaking if he didn't have Lanna to fill in the blanks when he lost his words. Honestly, I didn't think either of them could survive without the other.

I wondered what that felt like, finding someone who completed you so fully.

Not that I was looking for that.

"Considering we're in the middle of nowhere," I said to my newest companion, "I can actually say I'm surprised by your gala." While there were a lot of common folk in Sunday dresses and ill-fitting suit jackets, I could spy a good number of the upper class from where I stood. Whatever the painting was that Lanna drooled over, it was enough to bring out some of the better crowd.

The event planner smiled knowingly. "As a Davenport, I would imagine you've been to your fair share of events," he said.

I laughed. "I live at these events, Mr...."

"Giles. Hanson Giles."

"Davenport," I replied in the same haughty manner. "Catherine Davenport."

Across the ballroom, I thought I saw Matthew mouth an exaggerated something that looked a lot like, "Bond. James Bond," and then he winked at me and went back to staring me down. If he could tell what I was saying, even from that far away, there was no way I was going to be able to sneak out with one of the caterers like I was hoping. The moment I started talking to someone I shouldn't, Matthew would see right through it and swoop in to stop me. I needed another plan.

"So what's this famous painting you have featured tonight?" I asked Giles, tucking my arm in his and nudging him in the direction of the display. "I'll admit, I don't know much about art." On the rare occasion I did go to events like this, I usually spent them in back hallways with whomever I found first.

Giles smiled, but there was something off about it, just like it was strange that he held his arm so stiffly, as if he was nervous. I made plenty of men nervous, but I was barely flirting at this point, and I doubted he would go for it even if I was trying harder. Not when Adam was his boss. So what was making him so jumpy? "Gustav Klimt was one of Austria's most famous artists," he said as he glanced quickly at his watch. "We recently discovered this work of his that was previously unknown, and we decided to unveil it to the world in a smaller setting than we normally would have. For several reasons, but primarily because Mr. Munroe insisted on it."

That wasn't surprising, given the way Lanna couldn't stop glancing at the painting. And while I couldn't see what the big deal was—it looked like someone had scribbled it with crayon—I was a bit distracted by the way Giles wouldn't even look at it. And for an event planner, he was oddly pleased by the small setting. I would have thought he'd want bigger and better.

"How much is it worth?" I asked Giles as I glanced around the ballroom and tried to find anything else out of place. Maybe this guy was just a nervous sort of person.

His smile grew bigger, and I could recognize greed when I saw it. It was the same look everyone had in my world. "I'm hoping it'll be worth at least $300 million."

I felt my jaw drop. Even for me, that was a whole lot of money. "Adam can sell that thing for that much?" I asked. So maybe my cousin-in-law wasn't *completely* middle class and boring.

Giles chuckled. "Soon we'll be crowning a new King of Art, but time will tell us if he actually manages to get back what he paid for this particular piece."

A shiver ran up my spine. Even if he really was uncertain Adam could make a profit by selling the painting, that was sure an odd way to put it. When Giles glanced at me, I put on a smile, but I wasn't entirely sure if I could trust this event planner. "How long have you been working for Adam?" I asked him and continued my search of the crowds. Generally, the guests seemed happy to just mill about and talk while they sipped their drinks and viewed the other artwork, and the only other people in the room seemed to be caterers, all of them slipping through the crowds with trays of food and champagne.

Most of them, at least.

There were a couple of caterers who held empty trays but didn't seem to be in a hurry to head to the kitchen to reload.

"It's been a while," Giles said, and he couldn't fully hide a bit of bitterness in his voice, though he certainly tried. "Would you like to know about any more of the paintings, Miss Davenport?"

No, I wanted to see why that scruffy-looking caterer in the corner was watching Adam so intently.

"Planning an escape?" a voice said behind me, and I jumped. Matthew narrowed his eyes a little as I turned to meet his gaze.

"No," I said quickly. "Matthew, I think there's something—"

"Cut the crap, cuz," he replied and wrapped his fingers around my arm in a surprisingly strong grip. "I know a wannabe runaway when I see one."

The suspicious caterer was making his way toward the kitchen now, but he didn't seem to be in much of a hurry. Nothing about him seemed all that professional, from the way he held his tray with both hands to his too-long hair and scruffy beard. The rest of the catering staff were top notch.

"Matthew, I'm not escaping," I tried, though I wasn't sure how to clue him in with Giles standing right there and looking at me like I might know too much already. He was definitely in on the scheme, whatever the scheme was. "I'm just—"

Matthew wouldn't let me pull myself free, no matter how hard I tried. How stupid could he be? "Maybe we should go stand over with Lanna and Adam," he suggested. "Mr. Giles, thanks for giving her an art history lesson, but I can take it from here."

Giles was way too relieved to be free of the pair of us, and I couldn't understand how Matthew didn't see it. He had the same look my classmates had when they wanted to take something from someone else, which happened way more than it should have among the rich. Clearly having everything wasn't enough. Instead of recognizing the greed in Giles's eyes, my cousin pulled me across the ballroom toward the rest of our family as if I were some toddler causing trouble.

"There's something fishy going on," I said quietly. If he heard me, he ignored me. "I think someone might be—"

"Hey, sis," Matthew said to Lanna when we reached her. "I think our dear cousin is bored, so I thought maybe you might want to tell her why art is so important."

Lanna seemed completely caught off guard, and she held a little tighter to Adam's arm. "What? Right now?" She hadn't even touched the glass of champagne she held, and I was tempted to grab it and down it before she could remind me—again—I wasn't old enough to drink. This whole evening was getting ridiculous.

But I thought of a better option that wouldn't get me into even more trouble. "I have to go to the bathroom," I said as bluntly as I could. I had to get closer to the kitchen and find out where that fake caterer was going. I knew none of them would believe me if I tried to tell them why. "I'm guessing I need a babysitter for that?"

Lanna and Matthew exchanged looks, but to her credit, she shook her head. "Of course not," she said gently. "But I could use a break too, so I'll come with you."

Of course. Resisting the urge to roll my eyes, I let her take my hand and lead me to the hallway where the bathrooms were. At least we were in the right place now, and she would be a lot easier to ditch than Matthew.

The problem was the caterer was nowhere in sight, and there was a high chance I'd already lost him. *If something goes wrong,* I thought to myself, *I'm blaming Matthew.*

"Actually," Lanna said when we reached the hallway, "I don't think I have to go anymore. I'll just wait for you here, okay?"

"Fine," I snapped, though I probably should have been kinder if I didn't want her to suspect anything. At least this way I had a whole hallway to explore, and I could probably get through the kitchen if I had to escape the building. Poor Lanna might be waiting for me for quite a while, though I figured that was better than letting someone rob her of her precious painting.

Why else would someone be pretending to be a caterer? That was what I needed to find out.

The kitchen doors were at the end of the hallway, but there were several others along the hall that could have hidden any number of things, from supply closets to security rooms to offices. The bathrooms were clearly marked, as was the janitorial closet, and though there was a chance the shifty caterer was hiding in one of those rooms, I figured it would be better to check on some of the unmarked doors first, in case they were storerooms with other artifacts or whatever.

Just as I was about to pull on the first door, the fake caterer slipped out of the kitchen and into the next room over without even a glance down the hallway. I didn't have to think long to realize he was most likely about to do whatever it was that was going down, so I hurried down the hall and grabbed hold of the door before it closed, slipping inside the dark room before anyone saw me.

The room was full of computer monitors, and though the lights were off, there was enough light coming from the screens to illuminate the caterer, who hunched over a keyboard and typed something I couldn't read. They also revealed a security guard slumped unconscious against the wall beneath the desk.

Suddenly dizzy, I stepped back toward the door and fumbled for the handle before he noticed me. Cold metal met my fingers, and I turned the handle slowly, refusing to look away from the guy as he kept typing code into the command box on the screen. If I could just get back out into the hallway, I could grab Matthew and somehow convince him that—

The door latch clicked as I turned it, and the man froze at the same time I did.

Oh crap.

He turned his head slowly, completely tense, but the second he saw me, he relaxed a little. "You're not supposed to be in here," he said. He was abnormally tan, and up close I could tell it had been a while since he'd had a haircut. And while he wasn't particularly tall, his bulk suggested he had a lot of muscle underneath that ill-fitting catering uniform. I might have called him handsome in a different situation, but I couldn't see past the coldness in his brown eyes or the way he seemed to size me up just like I did him.

I figured I had two choices: I could try my luck at talking my way out of the situation and pretend I had no idea what he was doing there, or I could run. I knew my strengths, and I knew running in these heels wouldn't get me very far very fast. *Option A it is.*

I smiled, straightened up to my most flattering stance, and without letting go of the door I glanced around the room. "Oh," I said, keeping my voice as husky as I could, "I thought this was the little girl's room. Though…" *Time to work my magic.* "Maybe it's not a bad thing I ended up in the wrong place. What's your name, handsome?"

Without looking away from me, he typed the last few things he needed then hit enter and stood up straight. His grin sent a chill through me when he took a step closer. "Does that actually work for you?" he asked, cocking his head a little more with each step. "People buy that?"

My stomach twisted. Maybe Option B would have been a better choice. "Um." I pulled the door open, but he was close enough that he reached out a gloved hand and pushed it shut, at the same time grabbing my clutch—phone included—from my other hand and setting it on the desk. "I should really get back to…" Oh God, was that a gun at his waist?

He smiled wider, following my eyes to the weapon. "Here's how this is going to go, Princess," he said. "You've seen my face, so I really can't let you go."

Of all the times for Matthew to not be staring me down, why did it have to be now? Why couldn't he have just believed me when I told him something was up? "I won't tell anyone," I said, but I'd lost all confidence in my voice and sounded like a scared little girl, which probably wasn't all that far from the truth.

He shook his head. "That's not how this works. So be a good girl and don't make too much of a struggle, and I won't have to kill you and make more of a mess than there needs to be. Got it?"

Dizziness washed over me as I stood there against the door and tried to find a way out of this. I always found a way out. But I couldn't think of a single thing I could do that wouldn't get me shot and killed, so I nodded and fought back tears. I was stronger than that, and crying wouldn't help me anyway. This guy probably had no sympathy for tears.

"You're going to walk to the kitchen," the man instructed and grabbed his gun from his belt. "If you make any sudden moves, I *will* shoot you, but it doesn't have to come to that if you don't want it to."

Of course I didn't want it to come to him shooting me point blank. "I won't," I whispered and held my hands up, just to show him.

My one prayer was that someone would be out in the hallway and see me being held at gunpoint, but when we stepped through the door, the place was empty. I could hear voices from the gala, but I knew that even if I screamed, I'd be dead before anyone came to my rescue. Even when I reluctantly walked into the kitchen, my captor's hand tight around my arm, I could tell the caterers inside were too good at their jobs and actively ignored us as we passed them. I knew from experience it took a lot more than a few pointed glances to catch their attention.

"Through the door," the man said.

A wave of frigid air hit me hard as we stepped into the darkness outside, and I instinctively curled my free arm around myself. My coat was all the way at the front of the venue, on the other side of all the people who wouldn't wonder where I was until it was too late.

Suddenly a scream pierced the air, and I turned back toward the building. The man wrapped his arm around my chest to keep me from seeing much, but I did notice the whole building had gone dark and more than one person was spilling from the front door in the distance.

"White van," he hissed in my ear and shoved me forward.

Another man jumped out from the driver's seat as we approached and pulled open the back doors, and though he glanced at me with curiosity, I knew without trying he wouldn't help me. "Get in," he said to both me and my captor. "The others are almost here."

My kidnapper lifted me up and tossed me inside, and I landed on the hard floor with a gasp of pain. I barely had time to try to get up before he grabbed me again and flipped me onto my back, a length of rope in his hands.

"Please," I begged as he tied my wrists together. "You don't have to—"

"Shut up," he spat and shoved me deeper into the van.

Two others, black masks over their heads, suddenly leapt into the back, and at the same moment, the driver revved the engine and peeled off before the doors even closed. One man had a box tucked under his arm, and as his companion settled on one of the side benches that lined the back of the van, he gently rested the thin box against his legs.

"Everything good?" my captor asked roughly.

"What took you so long to kill the power?" the one with the box replied.

"A little complication," my captor said and jerked his head toward me.

My breath caught in my throat, my head spinning and my heart racing as three sets of eyes locked onto me.

"What the hell, Geller?" the one with the box practically spat.

"Who is she?" the other asked, and he inched a little closer to get a better look at me.

No way was I going to let any of them touch me. I would fight until my last breath, rather die than let them do anything to me.

My kidnapper—Geller—shrugged as he reached for the box. "She saw my face, Will. I couldn't let her go." And then from the box he pulled out the painting Adam's company debuted, the one by Klimt. The one worth millions.

I was right. I'd caught on to a heist. And I knew Geller's face, which meant I was a liability. They were going to kill me.

"She's gonna faint," one man said, his voice muffled.

"Quick, someone…"

CHAPTER FOUR

My head felt like it was wedged between two rocks. Every time my heart beat, it pounded against the rocks and sent a wave of pain through me. What a horrifying dream. Maybe if I told Matthew about it, he'd find a way to make me laugh about it. He was good at that.

Ugh, my whole body ached like I'd spent a cycle in a washing machine. Had I found some hard alcohol last night and drunk myself into a stupor? Probably. It wouldn't be the first time.

"Storm's getting closer," a deep voice muttered. "If we can't get this thing across state lines before tomorrow, we're dead."

"We'll be fine," another replied. "Geller's got this planned to every detail."

Geller. A shudder ran through me that had nothing to do with the frigid air. Not a dream.

The voices stopped when a moan slipped from my mouth, and I opened my eyes to find two blurry forms nearby. Where had they taken me? I blinked away unwanted tears and tried to clear my vision, but the warehouse full of boxes and crates didn't make me feel any better. Neither did the two men hunched over a table piled with maps. One was the driver, his wild hair tumbling around his shoulders as he leered at me. The other was younger, less than thirty, and didn't frighten me nearly as much. His eyes almost looked kind as he watched me.

I distrusted him immediately.

"You're awake," the younger said, making his companion roll his eyes.

"Of course she is, idiot," the driver said.

"You should tell Geller she's up," the other continued. "I'll explain the situation to her."

But the driver didn't move, his leer turning into a glare that made me shrink as far back into the hard couch as I could. "She doesn't need to know anything, Will," he argued. "You've obviously never dealt with a hostage before."

For the first time, the one named Will looked a little angry. "I've never had to because I do my job like I'm supposed to," he growled. "Now go get Geller. Giles should be contacting us any minute."

I was right. The theft had been an inside job, and Hanson Giles had made a poor career decision and chosen to help a bunch of thieves instead of stick with a multi-million-dollar art dealer. What an idiot.

Though he clearly didn't like being ordered around, the driver gave me one last examining glance before he turned and disappeared around a shelf of boxes, leaving me alone with the admittedly handsome thief who watched me just as intently as I stared at him. He really didn't look like a criminal, his curly black hair and gentle brown eyes making him look younger than he probably was. And so far he had stayed at his table rather than coming any closer. But I knew better than to trust a first impression when it came to men.

"How are you feeling?" he said after a moment, and then to my horror he approached me. I tried to scoot out of his reach, but he took hold of my bound hands anyway. "Easy," he said, as if I would believe him. "I'm not going to hurt you."

"Let me go," I said. "I won't tell anyone."

And to my surprise, he untied the rope from my wrists then stepped back, his hands in the air. What kind of trick was he playing? "This wasn't supposed to happen," he said.

He wasn't making any sense, and I rubbed the soreness from my wrists as I continued to watch him. Was he trying to lull me into a false sense of security before he did something to me? If that was the case, he was doing a terrible job at it. My experience with men told me they cared about two things in life: easy pleasure and not getting into trouble. Whatever this guy wanted, he could have taken it without untying my hands.

"I'm sorry," he said when I stayed silent. "If I had known, I might have…" He groaned and rubbed his face. "I need you to listen to me very carefully," he said then glanced behind him, making sure we were alone. He stepped closer again, and though I flinched, he just crouched next to me so he could whisper, "My name is William Dunn. I work for the San Francisco Police Department, and I've been undercover with Geller's California crew for over a year."

Could I really believe that? Probably not. But I didn't have much of a choice. So far this guy seemed a whole lot nicer than the others, and I didn't have many other options. Even if I slipped through the other door that was partially hidden on the far side of the room, I probably couldn't get far before the whole gang found me and decided I wasn't worth keeping alive.

"Can you get me out of here?" I whispered. "Please."

But his expression darkened, and he searched the warehouse again for signs of his partners. "That's the tricky part," he replied. "I have no way to contact my department; Geller jams all signals in case we try to turn on him. And I can't leave until I figure out his big play. I'm close, but not close enough. This is the first time he's been in the country in months."

My barely hopeful heart sank. "So I'm going to die here," I said.

"No," was Will's emphatic reply. "Not as long as I'm here."

"What can you possibly do?" I moaned. If he couldn't even get in touch with his alleged department, what good was he?

"What's your name?" he asked.

I clamped my mouth shut, knowing my name was more valuable than the diamond earrings I was wearing.

But to my horror, another voice answered the question for me: "Her name is Catherine Davenport," a rough-looking man said as he rounded the shelves, Geller right behind him. "People were talking about her all night."

Geller's eyes were bright with excitement. "As in Harris Davenport?"

"His niece," the other guy confirmed. "She could be worth a lot."

I wanted to jump up and strangle the guy, but I was distracted by Will swearing under his breath as he got to his feet. "This is a bad idea," he said. "The Davenports are way too powerful to—"

"I didn't ask for your opinion, Johnson," Geller growled, his eyes locked on me. "So you're more than just a pretty face, aren't you?" he asked me.

The smart thing would be to deny who I was, but I had a feeling Geller would believe his own man a lot more than he would believe me. So I did the next best thing and said, "My father will find you," because that threat worked in nearly every situation I didn't want to be in. Especially with men. As soon as I'd had my fun, I generally hit them with my father's identity or the fact I was still a minor.

That second escape wouldn't work anymore, unfortunately.

Geller's sneer sent a shiver through me, and he stepped a little closer to me. "I'm counting on that, Princess," he said. "Seems I have some calls to make. Felix," he said, addressing the driver, "you're in charge of the search now while I sweet talk Dear Dad. Johnson, make sure she doesn't go anywhere."

The last thief was still looking at me, and he grabbed Geller's arm. "What about Giles? He's asking when he'll—"

"He'll get his cut as soon as we make the sale," Geller muttered, looking at me again. "Tell him he'd better keep his alibi in check, or he's out. And make sure he has no idea about the girl, or things'll get more complicated than I want to deal with."

He snapped a quick picture of me with his phone, and then I watched the three of them leave the room, trying to come up with a good way to get out of here without running into any of them. Without knowing what the rest of the building was like, I highly doubted I could get far. I was pretty good at slipping away from chaperones for the most part, but this was on a whole different level. Besides, I still had no idea if I could actually trust Will.

Once we were alone, the cop seemed to relax just a bit and leaned against the table. "Okay," he said, probably to himself. "We can work with this."

"What now?" I asked him, hoping I could get some kind of clue about his loyalties.

He shrugged. "I don't know."

"For someone who claims to be a cop," I grumbled, "you're not exactly helpful."

Though he glared at me, it wasn't all that strong. "Geller will take his time," he said, though yet again I was pretty sure he was talking to himself. "You're valuable enough for him to think this through before he makes any real moves, but if he looks into your dad too much, this could get really ugly really fast."

I stared at him. Clearly he knew more about my family than the others, and I wasn't sure if that was a good thing or a bad thing. "Why?" I asked. Dad probably wouldn't even answer his phone. Before he left on his honeymoon, he told me not to bother calling because he wasn't planning to pick up the phone for anything. If I got myself into trouble, I would have to get myself out of it. But this wasn't exactly getting caught shoplifting from Tiffany's. This was a literal life or death situation. Was that what Will meant? That my dad wasn't the ransom-paying type?

Will shook his head, looking down at the many papers littering the table. "There's nothing Geller likes more than targeting a government official," he said, his voice low.

Dad worked for the government. I had no idea what he did or what department, because he had always refused to tell me, but if Will was saying what I thought he was saying, Geller was likely more dangerous than just an art thief. But how dangerous?

"Our best option is to get you away from him," Will continued, now more focused on something on the table. "As long as he can't find you, he can't hurt you or use you for leverage."

"So grab the keys and drive me back to Tahoe," I said, knowing it was likely more complicated than that. *Ugh, why did it have to be Tahoe?* If I had just gone to the Bahamas like I wanted, I wouldn't have ended up in this mess.

He shook his head and grabbed a pencil. As he traced a line along a map in front of him, he said, "If I leave, especially now, Geller will think I've run off with tonight's score, and he'll pack up and vanish, with or without whatever else he's here for. And until I figure out what it is he's looking for..." He trailed off, squinting at the map. "I can't afford to lose the tentative trust I have with him, and I definitely can't afford to scare him out of California again."

"Even if it saves my life?" I asked under my breath.

Catching something in my expression, Will grimaced. "I know I sound horrible," he said quietly, and, bringing the map with him, he came and sat next to me on the couch. "Geller is more dangerous than he seems, and we can't just give up. But I promise I will do everything I can to get you back home safe. We just have to be careful."

I liked to think I was pretty good at reading people. It was a necessary skill when my every move was watched and I had to know just how far I could push people in my favor before things went sour. I rarely made mistakes, so I rarely got myself into situations I couldn't get out of again. And though this felt like new territory, considering I'd never been kidnapped before, I was pretty sure I could trust Will the Cop.

"What do I need to do?" I asked. How, exactly, would he get me out of here?

Will thankfully kept his distance and sat just close enough to show me the map. "This road will lead you to a cabin," he said, just loud enough for me to hear. "If you follow it exactly and don't leave the cabin until I come find you, you should be safe."

Well that sounded like a terrible idea. "A cabin?" I asked, resisting the urge to raise my eyebrow and question his intelligence. That wouldn't exactly help me in this situation. "Whose cabin? How do you know no one will find me?"

"Because it's my cabin," he said patiently. "None of these people know my real name, so they wouldn't have any idea to look for it. I haven't been there for a few months, but there should still be some food and supplies up there, everything you'll need. Here's the code to turn on the power." He scribbled a few digits on the top of the map.

If I didn't know there were a few unsavory thieves somewhere nearby, I would have flat out refused. The Shack had been bad enough; a cabin in the woods screamed horror movie, and I was way too pretty to die this young. But I could tell even without trying the refusal route that this was probably my only option. I sighed and pulled the map a little closer so I could examine it. "How do I get there?" I asked. "Do I take the van and—"

"You'll have to walk," he replied, wincing when I sent him an involuntary glare.

"Walk," I repeated.

"I wish I could say it will be easy," he said, "but you're not exactly dressed for the occasion, and the only thing I can give you is a flashlight, though I highly suggest not using it if you can help it." He pulled the little cylinder from his jacket pocket and held it out to me. "Good luck."

It felt like the room spun in a full circle, leaving me almost too dizzy to sit up straight. "Wait," I gasped. "You want me to go *now*?" I hadn't even had a chance to psych myself up let alone study the map for a few minutes so I didn't get lost along the way. I wasn't exactly an expert navigator, and Will's trail didn't even follow a paved road. "You're insane."

Shushing me, Will winced again and put his hand over mine. "The longer you wait, the harder it will be. Geller can't ask a ransom or worse if he doesn't have the girl."

He can't get one if she's dead either. I didn't like to admit my shortcomings, few though they were, but, "Will, I can't do this. I can't trek across a mountain in heels and a dress."

"You can absolutely do it," he replied and gave my hand a squeeze. "And I'll come up to the cabin as soon as I can to get you home. I promise."

Then—I blamed the adrenaline—I grabbed his collar and pulled him in for a kiss as if I wasn't in any hurry to get away. And while I prided myself on my ability to kiss, I didn't expect to leave him looking completely bewildered. "Will?" I whispered. Maybe it hadn't been the best idea, but I needed at least something to feel normal before I marched off to my frigid death.

He blinked. "Hit me," he said.

"What?"

Shaking his head, as if to clear a fog, he crossed over to the nearest shelf and grabbed a large metal pipe. "We have to make your escape look authentic. So hit me." He held it out to me.

I'd had to hit many a man who didn't know when to keep his hands to himself, but this felt completely wrong. "I can't hit you," I protested. He was my only ally.

He put the pipe in my hand anyway and slipped out of his coat, setting it on the couch next to me. "Just hit me hard," he said and tensed. "I'd prefer it if you only had to hit me once."

I understood why I had to do it, but that didn't mean I wanted to. "Will."

A voice carried around the corner, and Will turned in alarm. My instinct was a little more reactive. In my panic, I swung the pipe as hard as I possibly could, and it collided with Will's head with a sickening crack. He crumpled in a heap almost immediately.

"Oh my God," I gasped, dropping the pipe at my feet. In the next second, I realized I had to run. Grabbing the map, flashlight, and Will's coat, I rushed straight for that partially hidden side door and out into the night.

"Okay," I told myself. "I can do this. I can do this."

I knew I probably didn't have much time before someone found Will, so I fumbled open the map and used the building's dim yellow light to look at the path Will had drawn for me.

"I can't do this," I said almost immediately.

It was completely dark outside. I had no idea where we were, or how far this supposed cabin was, or how to figure out which direction I had to go. His pencil trail looked like it went straight up the mountain, directly through trees and over rivers and miles of miles of wilderness. That was probably an exaggeration, but that still didn't mean I liked my odds. There was no way.

A gust of frigid wind cut through the thin fabric of my dress and carried with it the first flakes of a snowfall, and I realized this was the *only* way. If I tried to take the road back to town, Geller would find me immediately, just like if I stayed put. Either I would die here, or I could die trying to get away and take charge of my own fate.

"Look after yourself," I reminded myself as I pulled on Will's coat. Just like I did every time I came across a trial.

Basing my initial direction on the road on the other side of the warehouse, I set off into the nearby trees and prayed I wasn't making a terrible mistake.

* * *

I'd never hated snow more in my life. It kept my toes frigid and turned to ice beneath my feet and made following Will's path almost impossible, though I did my best. At every ridge, I double checked the map and prayed I knew enough about cartography to get myself where I needed to go. That was the least of my worries at the moment, though. My shoes were useless and stabbing straight into the frozen snow. My dress caught on bushes and tore around my legs, and Will's jacket was less of a coat than I would have liked.

Will had sent me out here to die, and I would have none of that.

"You can do this," I told myself as I stumbled up the mountain, my voice shaking. I had to be more convincing than that if I wanted to believe myself. "You are Catherine Freaking Davenport. You walked a Parisian runway when you were thirteen. You convinced Tom Cruise on Twitter to make another Mission Impossible. You spent three days partying in Singapore without sleeping. You can do anything!"

Except maybe trek up a mountain in the dark.

My unbidden tears were freezing to my cheeks, my fingers numb and my lungs heaving and my hair tangling in branches. This was nothing like a fashion show catwalk. Nothing like Chamonix.

"Come on, Catherine," I whispered. "You can't just give up." I didn't give up. I was the most stubborn person I knew. If I gave up now, everything I'd done in my life, everything I had worked for, everything I had become, was for nothing. I didn't teach myself how to run the world for nothing.

"Be the badass bitch I know you are."

But a gust of wind knocked me off balance. I fell against a tree, the bark clawing at my skin as I clung to the trunk to keep myself on my feet. The storm was getting worse. The snow fell too thick, too fast. I couldn't see.

Grabbing the map, I shone the flashlight and tried to figure out how much farther. I had already crossed that stream and climbed the rise above it, but I'd gotten so cold over the last couple hours that I had forgotten to count my steps or try to notice the landscape around me. It was too dark. Too cold.

I thought about giving up. Sitting down next to the sappy tree and letting the snow engulf me. It was the middle of the night, and I was exhausted, and no one would blame me for being a realist and recognizing I was going to die anyway. So why bother dragging it out? No one was going to miss me anyway.

I slapped myself for that thought. "Of course they're going to miss you," I scolded, though my lips were too cold to form the words clearly. "The whole damn world loves you, Catherine Davenport. They all want to be you."

A sob wrenched from my lungs. I hated when people lied to me, especially when the liar was me.

Maybe I could go just a little bit longer. Just a little.

I made it three steps and slipped.

"I can't do this. I can't."

Two more steps. Everything ahead of me was dark behind the falling snow. So dark.

I struggled back to my feet. *Too dark.* There was something there.

A cabin. I stumbled forward. And when I grabbed the doorknob, it turned, unlocked.

Could I have made it? I shoved my way through the door and slammed it shut behind me, cutting off the bitter chill and the noise of the wind and the terror that I would freeze to death in the middle of a California forest. I couldn't hold myself up anymore, and I fell against the door, my tears suddenly hot on my cheeks and my lungs gasping to breathe just a little. Just enough to survive.

"This is not what I expected to wake up to."

I didn't have the energy to scream, but what little air I did have disappeared at the sound of a man's voice somewhere close. The room was too dark. All I saw was a shadow smaller than the others, one that moved just a little, enough to tell me I was not as alone as I wanted to be. I'd escaped one nightmare and traded it in for another. Was there nowhere safe?

"You a friend of Will's?" the voice asked.

I sank to the floor, my tears doubling as the smallest of hopes crept into my heart. Had I found the right place? "Will," I confirmed, unable to say anything else. My eyes adjusted to the darkness, enough to see that the small shadow was a man lying on a couch. Dim light from the windows reflected off his eyes as he watched me sob by the door, and he hadn't yet moved any closer to me. That, at least, was a good sign.

Finding what strength I could, I gripped the flashlight and clicked it on, shining it directly on his face.

"Easy," he mumbled, but I didn't lower the light.

Seeing his details didn't reassure me at all.

I guessed he was in his mid-twenties, around the same age as Will, and I had no idea how long he'd been lying there. Beneath the thin blanket that barely covered his bulk, his clothes were wrinkled and worn, the smell of him becoming almost overpowering the longer I sat there. Dark circles rimmed his eyes that shone out from his pale skin, and several days' scruff covered the lower half of his face. A tattoo poked out from the collar of his tan t-shirt, but I couldn't tell what it was. Overall, he looked homeless or worse, and I clutched the flashlight a little tighter. I didn't have the strength to fight him off if he came for me.

"I know I don't look great," he muttered, his eyes drooping with sleepiness even as he fought to see through the flashlight. "I wasn't expecting company, and I don't have the code to turn the water or power on. Is Will with you?"

I fought back another wave of tears, shaking my head as I moved the flashlight to take in the rest of the room. A fireplace sat cold and empty across from the couch, and a dining table waited behind the sofa. A small kitchen was barely visible on the far wall from the door, and a little hallway led farther into the cabin, probably to a bedroom or two. The whole place smelled musty and dank, and I wondered if Will had really been here within the last few months or if he had only said that to make me feel better about coming here.

Would he ever come back to the cabin and get me back home?

"Are you ever going to say anything?" the man asked, drawing my light back to him. "Or are you just going to sit there and pretend I'm speaking nonsense? *Parlez-vous français? Hablas español? A ty govorish' po russki? Sen Türkçe konuşmayı biliyor musun? Nagsasalita*—"

"Shut up," I groaned and pressed a hand to my forehead, closing my eyes tight and trying to stop my heart from racing. I needed to calm down. I needed to think. And I couldn't do that if I had a massive man spewing a million different languages at me. I could understand looking Russian—I'd been mistaken for a Russian model before—but I had no idea why he would think I was Filipino. "Who even are you?"

I heard him shift on the couch, the floor creaking beneath him. His response came out a little breathless: "I'm Seth. Will's friend. Is he…?"

I shrugged, letting the flashlight fall onto the wood floor next to me with a clunk. The light spun a few times, flashing through my eyelids. I was exhausted. Physically. Mentally. Emotionally. The last time I'd been this tired, I'd just spent a weekend with a rather handsome young British ambassador on a thrilling romp around Rome.

"Well," Seth continued, and I looked up just as he settled deeper beneath his blanket, "you'd better hope he comes soon, or you'll be spending a long time on that cold floor, Princess."

Princess. How many times had someone called me that? Too often to count, and it brought a surprising smile to my face. I *was* a princess. Maybe not literally, but I knew I deserved everything that came to royalty, which meant I couldn't sit on this floor forever. Taking a deep breath, I slowly picked myself up off the floor, bringing the flashlight with me. I'd gotten this far on my own, hadn't I? I didn't need Will to come rushing in and save me. I just needed to find the place to turn on the power, and then I could use the phone hanging on the wall in the kitchen and call in the cavalry.

There was a metal panel on the wall next to the ancient refrigerator, and inside sat a keypad. I typed in the numbers Will had written, praying he really was my ally, and to my utter relief the whole cabin shuddered to life around me, though it sounded a bit like it didn't want to wake up. A generator sputtered somewhere below, and the smell of burning dust filled the air as the heater tried to warm up a poorly insulated room.

As the lights flickered on in the main room, I glanced at the man on the couch and wrinkled my nose. The added illumination didn't do him any favors as he in turn examined me with bleary, sleep-deprived eyes. Now that I could see him, I almost wished I couldn't. His face was bruised in places, though based on their yellowish tint they were a few days old, and he had a half-healed split on his lip. Despite his lack of any sort of hygiene and hair that was just a bit too long, he had a very military look about him. I'd seen plenty of soldiers wandering about Washington D.C. while I went to school there, and Dad had had his fair share of military visitors over the years.

If I had to guess, Seth was a soldier, and I couldn't decide if that made me want to trust him more or less.

"So you came with power," Seth said. "Did you also come with a name?"

My name was apparently worth more than I'd thought, so I didn't think it was a good idea to tell him what it was. So I told myself to lie. "Catherine," I said. *Lie better.*

His mouth quirked in a slight smile. "You got a last name to go with that, Catherine?"

I narrowed my eyes. "Do you, Seth?"

His smile seemed to grow ever so slightly, but that was the only part of him that moved. He barely breathed as he lay there. "Touché," he muttered and closed his eyes, signaling the much wanted end of our conversation.

I had no intention of getting to know the man any more than I already had, no matter how long I was stuck there. The storm was getting worse outside, and I had a feeling it was going to be a while before I could get out of this place and back to my life. So it seemed it was time to explore and make sure I could actually survive in this place, assuming the man on the couch let me survive.

This is going to be fun.

CHAPTER FIVE

The phone didn't work. I guessed there was too much interference from the storm, and the line just crackled when I tried to dial, so I searched for some other way to improve my situation. The cabin had all of three rooms: the front room, which I vowed to avoid as much as possible; a bathroom, which thankfully had hot water as soon as the crippled system managed to heat it; and a bedroom, where I locked myself in and tried not to fall back into panic. I found some clothes in the closet that hopefully belonged to Will and changed out of my dress. They were obviously too big, but I managed to wear with a little adjustment so the pants didn't slip off. It was better than being stuck in an evening gown that was torn and muddied and soaking wet.

Once I had thick wool socks on my frozen feet, I slid beneath the covers of the bed and curled into a ball to stay warm as the wind howled louder and louder outside. At this point, that snow was the one thing keeping me in the cabin, since I was smart enough to know I couldn't just wander around an unfamiliar place when a literal blizzard was raging. As soon as it stopped, though, I was out of there. Whether or not Will was going to come to my aid.

If only I could stay warm… I gathered up every blanket I could find, but even then, the bedroom had a chill hanging over it I couldn't hide from. As I lay there shivering and wishing the heater was actually functional, I couldn't help but think about the gas fireplace back at The Shack, the one Matthew kept on to keep the cold out. I'd never fully appreciated fire until that moment. There was a fireplace out in the main room, but Seth was also in that room, and I had little hope of convincing him to switch places with me when he had clearly spent a good deal of time on that couch and didn't seem inclined to move.

I only lasted a couple of hours before I couldn't handle it anymore. Gathering up two of my blankets and keeping them wrapped tight around my shoulders, I slowly ventured out of the bedroom and into the front room. *Of course.* Seth hadn't moved, and I could have sworn the smell around him had gotten worse. "You can take a shower now," I growled at him as I passed to the fireplace.

He acknowledged the reminder with a grunt, not even bothering to open his eyes.

Crouching down, I searched for a switch or something to turn the fire on. It took me about twenty seconds to come to the horrifying realization that this fireplace required actual wood instead of a steady gas line, and I searched the dimly lit room for any logs or even a match. Nothing.

"There's a pile out front," Seth said quietly.

I stared at him, waiting for him to offer to go get some. But he was silent, and a sense of dread settled over me. So much for chivalry. I could take care of myself, but I had no intention of spending the whole storm catering to a lazy guy like Seth. I may have been stuck in a place even worse than Lanna and Adam's, but I still had my dignity. "What?" I snapped. "You expect me to do it? How about you be a man and do it yourself?"

He opened one eye, and I couldn't tell if he was grimacing or smiling. Either way, he didn't have a response to my request.

I folded my arms, though I was pretty sure I didn't look all that impressive drowning in a couple of patchwork quilts. "You're really going to sit there and do nothing?"

He gave me a sort of half shrug as his other eye opened to take me in. "You're the one who wants a fire," he said, hardly loud enough for me to hear it.

My jaw dropped, but anger flared up inside me. Fine. If I could convince a senator's son to sneak me into the White House, I could carry in some firewood. Leaving one blanket around my shoulders, I tossed the other one over Seth's head so he couldn't just sit there and watch me brave the snow just so I wouldn't freeze to death. How was he not cold, anyway, with nothing but that tiny little blanket over him?

The wind blasted the door open as soon as I turned the handle, and I left it wide open just to spite the irritating jerk on the couch. If he was so warm, he could handle a little cold as I did all the hard work. Night had fallen thick, but luckily a light glowed orange on the porch that wrapped around the side of the cabin. At least Will had given me a way to turn the power on, but I wished he could have found a different way to get me to safety. I wasn't sure how long I could really do this whole deserted cabin thing.

Well, I thought as I shuffled my stockinged feet through drifts of snow that were already collecting on the porch, *not as deserted as he probably expected.* Or had he known Seth would be here and sent me here anyway?

I found the pile Seth said would be there and clenched my jaw tight. I could do this.

Several splinters later and a few shrieks as I brushed away spider webs, I had a ridiculously heavy armful of wood and a face full of melting snow. I kicked the cabin door shut behind me and tried not to even look at the jackass as I dropped the logs next to the fireplace. I would find some matches in a minute, but first I had to deal with my hands. They stung with cold and wood slivers, and I hoped the bathroom had some tweezers among the random supplies tossed in the cupboard drawers.

"The least you could do is light it," I snapped at the motionless man on the couch and stomped back to the bedroom to find some dry socks and see to my mangled hands.

Twenty minutes later, with dry clothes and bleeding but wood-free hands, I stared at my face in the bathroom mirror and fought back tears. I barely recognized myself. I'd cried away all my makeup already, but I used to look so confident. Radiant. Now I looked horrifyingly like Seth, dark circles under my eyes and my hair a jumbled mess and my skin pale. Even when I tried to smile and bring back some life into my face, I barely managed it. I wasn't even sure what time it was, but the art gala felt like days ago. That time had broken me in a way nothing ever had before.

Would I ever get back home? Really?

Grabbing my blanket, I shuffled back into the front room to search for some matches to light a fire, since there was little chance Seth had put in the effort. But to my surprise, the fireplace glowed with warmth that had already started heating up the little room. I turned to Seth, and though the only difference from before was he'd draped my abandoned quilt over himself, he had obviously gotten up to start the fire.

So he *was* cold. He kept his eyes closed, probably pretending to be asleep as I stood there staring at him.

"Good job," I said. "You finally figured out how to use your masculinity for something useful."

He opened one eye again, looking even more pale than before in the flickering orange light. And yet, true to nature, he said nothing.

That was going to get really old really fast. "Look," I said, folding my arms as I sat near the fireplace. Goodness, that was warm. Cozy. "If I'm going to be stuck here, I'm not going to act like some maid and do all the work. I'm better than that, and I'm not going to let you just sit around all day pretending to sleep when you're more suited for the stuff like bringing in firewood so we don't freeze. Could you at least change your clothes so you don't smell like something that came out of the gutter? I have gardeners who smell better than you."

He had both eyes open now, his expression decidedly blank considering what I was saying to him. "I liked you better when you didn't talk," he said, and his voice had gotten rough and husky. "A regular princess like you, I'm surprised you haven't threatened to call your lawyer yet and sue me for treating you unfairly."

"Don't be an idiot," I said. The phone didn't work.

"Can't stop who I am," he grunted and almost smiled. If he had done it properly, he might not have looked so frightening as he lay there.

"And who are you?" I asked.

"Seth," he replied.

"You've already said that."

"You've already asked that."

"You're Will's friend?" I asked, though I was really tempted to go back to ignoring him. Maybe I could find a way to get him outside and lock him out, and then I wouldn't have a constant fear in the back of my head that he was going to come after me as soon as I turned my back.

Seth blinked, which must have meant 'yes.' "We grew up together," he said. "Came to this cabin all the time when we were kids."

He had so little expression in his face and voice that it was pretty much impossible to know if he was lying. My only hope that he might have been telling the truth was the fact that he had mentioned Will's name before I did. "Why should I believe you?" I asked and grabbed a pillow that had probably fallen off the couch. As much as I didn't want to make myself any more vulnerable than I already was, I could barely hold my head up anymore.

If anything was going to happen to me, I wouldn't be able to stop it even if I was awake. Not unless I got some sleep.

Seth's lips quirked in another smile. "'Cause that storm is only getting worse, so you don't have much of a choice," he said and closed his eyes, apparently falling asleep a moment later.

I grabbed the heavy iron poker that sat near the fireplace, just in case, and I seemed to slip away the moment I touched my head to the pillow.

* * *

By the time I woke up, I'd had more than enough dreams of Geller and the rest of his crew bursting in through the cabin door with guns blazing and Will in a police uniform beaten to death on the floor. I wasn't sure how long I'd been tortured with those visions, but the windows were a little more white and a little less black. Morning must have come, though I was still so exhausted that I wasn't sure why I'd woken up aside from the fact that I was lying on a threadbare rug over a wood floor. I turned to the fire and found it barely glowing while the storm still raged outside. Another turn of my head told me Seth was still asleep.

"Shocking," I said out loud, though he didn't stir.

Thank goodness there was probably enough wood out there to last us a month, or I would have been worried by how quickly we'd gone through my first armful. This time when I gathered up wood, I used the blanket over my hands to keep from getting stabbed a hundred times with splinters. I couldn't hold as much that way, but at least I stayed clean and dry. The blanket wouldn't be as lucky, but I could just switch it with Seth's. He wouldn't notice.

"Next time, you're getting the wood," I declared loudly, dropping the logs on the floor and letting it crash so Seth couldn't possibly stay asleep.

He didn't move.

My anger building, I crossed over to him and grabbed his blankets, tearing them free so he could at least get a fraction of the cold shock I got going out onto the porch. But when Seth still didn't react, my heart started to pound in my chest as I stared at him lying there. Was he green? It was hard to tell. But sweat definitely bathed his pale face, and he shivered even though he barely breathed. What was…

My eyes locked on his stomach, where the entire lower half of his shirt was soaked with blood. I heaved, luckily coming up empty since I hadn't eaten anything since before the party. What the hell happened to him? Reaching out, I gingerly lifted his shirt and found a red-stained square of gauze taped to his belly, though it hardly seemed to do him any good. It wasn't the only wound, either, though the rest of the bruises and cuts around his body were partially healed. The one beneath the gauze was fresher. And bloodier. As much as I didn't want to look, I peeled the fabric away, revealing a ragged hole in his skin, oozing with pus and seriously inflamed.

"Dear God," I breathed, staring at it. How long had he been lying there on that couch? I retched again, falling to my knees next to him, and looked back up at his face. No wonder he hadn't bothered getting more wood when he was half dead already. Maybe worse. "You're lucky I've seen fourteen seasons of Grey's Anatomy," I told him with a humorless laugh, even though I was pretty sure he wasn't conscious enough to hear me. I needed to talk out loud before I went into a panic again, even if he wouldn't be able to talk back.

But a TV drama was nothing close to a medical degree, and I feared even that wouldn't be enough to help this guy.

* * *

It took an hour in the shower before I felt like I'd washed the blood from my hands. Or maybe it was because I was afraid to go back out into the front room. A sewing kit I found in the bathroom wasn't exactly medical standard, and I'd probably drunk more of the half empty bottle of vodka than I used for Seth's wound. If I went back out there and found him dead, I wasn't sure I could handle that when I'd barely managed to keep myself together up to this point. It didn't matter how many times I told myself I was strong and I'd handled worse.

I wasn't. And I hadn't.

Whether he'd been shot or stabbed, Seth had been dying, and he probably knew it. I didn't want to think about what that meant about the man trapped in this cabin with me, whether he was a criminal or simply in the wrong place at the wrong time. I didn't want to think about what Seth would have done if no one had shown up to join him at the cabin. Just died there on the couch and rotted away until spring?

More than once I was glad I hadn't eaten anything, but that didn't make me feel any less sick and weak.

Where was Will? Was the storm so bad that he couldn't even get up here? Or had something gone wrong? He hadn't said how long it would take to come meet me, and there was always that chance he figured I would be fine on my own and never come. Was he also lying dead on a couch because he didn't have someone like me there to try to save him?

When the warm water ran out, I had to leave the shower, though I wasn't sure I would be able to look at my hands the same way again. There was so much blood. So much infection. And I'd cleaned it as best I could, but would it be enough? Wrapping a towel around myself, I cleared a space in the mirror so I could get a look at my face. I hadn't thought it was possible, but I looked even worse than before. How much hell would I have to go through before I couldn't even recognize myself?

I couldn't stay in the bathroom forever. The steamy air was already cooling, and the snow pelted the window and made the little room feel smaller than I was comfortable with. I had to go out there sooner or later, so I took a deep breath and pulled open the door.

A hulking figure greeted me.

I shrieked, slamming the door shut and falling back against the shower door with my heart in my throat. Several seconds later, once I'd managed to breathe again, I gingerly reached for the door and pulled it open.

At least Seth looked repentant, though pain darkened his expression into a scowl that made me take a step back in wariness. I doubted he could have done anything to me, at least, considering he couldn't even stand up without leaning against the door frame. He barely looked any better than he had before, still sweaty and green, but at least he was standing. Maybe I'd helped him after all.

To his credit, he only once let his eyes stray to the fact I stood there in a towel. Aside from that discerning glance, he kept his eyes on mine. They were blue, I realized, an almost aqua color that practically glowed in the light from the bathroom. Opening his mouth, he took a shaky breath and spoke two words: "Thank you."

Before I could get over my shock, he turned and stumbled back to the couch where he collapsed and seemed to promptly fall asleep again.

I stayed bundled under blankets in the bedroom until my hair was dry, trying to figure out the man in the other room. Why wouldn't he tell me he was hurt? He had a pretty good reason to avoid going out for wood, so he could have said… Would I have believed him?

Probably not.

What sort of man didn't go straight to a hospital when he was hurt like that? Or maybe he was hurt *at* the cabin. Was I not safe here? Was some crazy man running around stabbing people in the woods? That was how it happened in all the horror movies, and I certainly felt like I was trapped in one. But no matter how or when he was hurt, it didn't explain why Seth wouldn't tell me about his wound when it was clearly killing him. His gratitude made me think he didn't want to die, but everything else he'd done made me wonder.

I curled up a little tighter, telling myself to ignore the chill just a little longer. I didn't think I was scared of Seth just yet, but that didn't mean I wouldn't be wary. Nor did it make me want to hang around him. Not until I figured out more about him, and the only way to do that was to be in the same room and hold a conversation with him. That, I decided, was not a good idea.

Only when my stomach growled a couple hours later did I crawl out of my cocoon, silently praying Will hadn't been mistaken when he said there would be food. Before now, I hadn't felt the least bit hungry, with fear and nausea eating away at my stomach, but quite suddenly I was ravenous.

Through the closed bathroom door I could hear the shower running, which meant I had a small amount of time with the kitchen to myself. And maybe once he was clean, it would be a little easier to be in the same room as Seth. I quickly added a couple more logs to the fire, and then I flipped on the light in the kitchen and began my search for something to eat.

The fridge, unfortunately, was empty. I found some precooked meat something in one of the cupboards, as well as some flour and sugar. Another cupboard held some dishes, and in the corner pantry I found a bunch of soup cans. That would work. While I'd never actually cooked for myself, Rachel Ray and I were online friends and I'd seen all her videos. How hard could it be, really?

Opening the can was my first obstacle, since I had no idea what I was doing. Though there were several utensils and tools, one of them probably designed specifically to open cans, I resorted to taking what

I was pretty sure was a knife sharpener and stabbing it into the top of the can enough times that I could shake most of the soup into a pot I found. I flipped one of the knobs on the stove to high, since I wasn't feeling very patient, and though I had expected flames to pop up, I quickly realized the stove was electric and hoped it would actually work and warm up the soup I put on top of it.

"Okay," I said, frowning at my sad attempt at feeding myself. How had I managed to go eighteen years without learning some basic survival skills? "This is looking right, at least."

Leaving the soup to heat—hopefully—I took to searching the cupboards for a bowl. The spoon I grabbed from a drawer looked questionable, so I grabbed some soap from under the sink and decided to wash everything before I used it, just in case. Stomach rumbling, I tried to be as meticulous as I could just so I wouldn't think too hard about how hungry I really was. Scrub, rinse, dry with a towel. Repeat. I kept up the routine until the stove hissed suddenly, along with a horrifying smell.

The soup was exploding! Bubbling up and out of the pot, the soup hit the red-hot burner below the pan and turned to instant smoke. I waved my arms around to get rid of the smoke before Seth came out of the shower and…

His laugh was deep. Hearty. And when I turned to face him with heat burning in my cheeks, I barely recognized him.

Standing there in a towel wrapped around his waist, Seth was…surprising. Alive. Now that he wasn't dying, there was a light in his eyes that hadn't been there before. Water dripped from his sandy hair onto his wide, bare shoulders, and he'd shaved, revealing a striking jaw. Every inch of him was made of muscle—literally—and his tattoo was in plain sight now, an image of two dog tags on a chain over his heart. That tattoo drew my eyes to his enormous chest and down to a ridiculously defined abdomen that was impressive even with the week-old injuries dotting his skin. He'd taken a plastic bag and taped it over the stitches I'd given him, and… And I stopped my eyes from going any farther.

There was no point in admiring the man when he was suddenly a threat again. Being no longer confined to the couch meant he wouldn't be as easy to get away from, and the guy was huge. He had to be at least six and a half feet tall and weighed twice as much as me, so I had to be careful.

Laughter still echoing in his smile, Seth came forward—I shrunk out of his way—and turned the stove off, lifting the still bubbling pot and dumping it in the sink. Then he gave me a look that made me want to crawl in a corner and die because I hadn't given anyone a reason to give me a look like that in years.

I was *not* a child.

"Wow," he said, gazing down at the soup as it disappeared down the drain. "I'm a little amazed you didn't burn the place down."

"I was hungry," I explained.

He raised an eyebrow and tightened his hold on his towel. "Yeah, I guessed that part. Have you ever actually cooked before, Princess?"

That name was going to get really old really fast. Especially when he said it like a bitter taste in his mouth. "Of course I have," I lied. "I got distracted."

He smiled a little then nodded his head toward the bedroom. "How about you go find me some of those clothes," he said, "and I'll cook us something edible."

In any other situation I would have told him it would be a shame to cover up a specimen like him, but I kept that thought to myself. "Fine," I said, letting him hear my annoyance for looking at me like I had no idea how to do anything.

Fifteen minutes later, I sat across the table from Seth and ate my soup in silence. I tried my best not to look up at him—his eyes were way too piercing—and he didn't feel the need to fill the space between us with talking. He just sipped his soup, every once in a while grunting in discomfort if he shifted wrong.

I wasn't used to silence. People loved to hear me talk, and I loved to talk about myself, and silence usually led to awkwardness and looking at each other a little too closely. I didn't like it, and once I finished my food—eating twice as fast as Seth—I decided I couldn't handle the quiet anymore.

"How did that happen?" I asked while he was checking on the bandage beneath his flannel shirt.

Seth looked up, meeting my eyes with an immediate scowl that set me on edge. "You don't need to know," he said, his voice low.

Well, if he was going to be a jerk about it, at least I knew how to hold my own. I'd spent my life around jerks. I could be just as stubborn as him, and I had developed a thick skin over the years. "Why not?" I asked. "I have a right to know why I needed to save your life."

He clenched his jaw, his eyes taking in my face. "Okay," he said, though he wasn't exactly pleased by the idea. "I was stabbed."

My heart did a little flip of fear. It wasn't like I hadn't guessed as much, but I didn't like hearing the confirmation. "By who?"

But he shook his head. "I can't tell you that."

Of course he couldn't. Especially if I was right about his occupation. "You're a soldier, aren't you?" I asked.

He gripped his spoon so hard it bent a little in his fist. "What makes you say that?" he asked, though he seemed to realize he had pretty much answered in the affirmative.

So I kept going, hoping to get more answers out of him so I wasn't stuck here so blind. "How did you end up here at Will's cabin?"

"I walked," he replied.

"After getting stabbed?"

There was that half shrug again. "That happened a few days ago," he said. His spoon was practically bent in half now as he waited for my interrogation to continue.

But I wasn't sure how to respond to that last comment. "How did you survive a few days looking like that?" I asked, trying hard to keep amazement out of my voice. I was no doctor, but he'd been seriously hurt. He couldn't even move from the couch except to light the fire, so how in the hell did he trek through a snowy forest while bleeding out?

"A doctor in Vientiane patched me up," he said then winced, probably because he hadn't meant to tell me *where* he was stabbed. He eyed me carefully, and I could guess he hoped I had no idea where that was.

"What were you doing in Laos?" I asked, pulling my eyebrows together.

Cursing under his breath, he repaired the damage to his spoon then ate a few spoonfuls of soup before he answered. "Army," was all he said.

"I figured that part out already, if you remember," I said with a roll of my eyes. "So you were doing Army stuff in Laos when you were stabbed? What sort of person uses a knife instead of a gun? Wouldn't that be easier?"

Lifting one eyebrow, he stared at me like he wasn't sure what I'd asked. "Would you prefer that I was shot instead?"

I scowled. "That's not what I meant, though it's not off the table. Why can't you tell me who stabbed you?"

"Because they might try again," he answered simply, and as I sat there in horror, he took another bite of soup like he hadn't said anything remotely shocking.

"Again?" I whispered. "But why…?"

"Because obviously it didn't work the first time."

How could someone talk about getting stabbed like it happened every day? What sort of stuff was Seth into that would lead him to the kind of person who would do that? There was something definitely wrong with this guy, and I watched him as I wondered how I managed to get trapped in a cabin with someone like him.

Rolling his eyes, Seth gripped his spoon again and mumbled, "That's not a good look for you, Princess."

"Don't call me that," I replied, equally annoyed by him as he obviously was by me. "You don't know anything about me."

His careful indifference shifted into something colder as he studied me across the table. I didn't normally mind people's inquisitive stares, but Seth seemed to look deeper, penetrating my defenses and seeing things I wasn't sure I wanted him, or anyone, to see. "Enlighten me," he said after a moment. "How did *you* end up here looking like you'd been dragged the whole way? I'm guessing it's not for a romantic getaway, and the only other thing I can figure is you're hiding from someone."

"Geller," I whispered, involuntarily shuddering. If not for him, I wouldn't be here at all. I would be back with my cousins, or maybe even on a plane to Cabo for a proper Christmas. Instead, I was stuck in a tiny cabin in the middle of a blizzard, with only a half-dead soldier with too many secrets to keep me company.

"As in Max Geller? How did you get mixed up with a white collar criminal?" Seth pressed.

I supposed it was only fair to return the favor and answer a few things, even if Seth hadn't given me much detail about his own situation. "I was attending a gala down by the lake," I said.

"Of course you were," came the mumbled reply.

"Geller was acting as a caterer, and I saw him sneak into a room he wasn't supposed to be in, so I followed him."

"Ridiculous move," Seth growled. If every other sentence I spoke was going to be punctuated with an underhanded remark, I wasn't going to tell him at all. I didn't need his company, nor did I want it. "Sorry," he said, sensing my growing irritation.

I wasn't sure I wanted to continue, thinking back on the events of the party. I'd never been so terrified in my life, and reliving it was almost as bad. "I saw his face," I whispered, "so Geller took me with him. Pressed a gun into my back and tossed me into his van. That's how I met Will."

"And he helped you escape," Seth offered, narrowing his eyes a little. "Do you realize how lucky you are he managed to be part of that crew? Will's been trying to find a way into Geller's crew for years. Since before he graduated the Academy. I don't know much about him, but according to Will, Geller's been a big deal for a long time. You're lucky to be alive."

Seth's commentary wasn't exactly making me feel any better about the situation. Will was my only connection to the outside world, my only hope, and obviously I didn't know him very well. I'd spent all of twenty minutes with the man, and I couldn't help but imagine him failing me and leaving me to die in the middle of nowhere.

All because Matthew wouldn't listen to me.

"Hey," Seth said gently. "The closest place Geller could be hiding out is miles from here. *Miles.* And you walked the whole way in heels and a ball gown. That's no small feat."

Was he seriously trying to make me feel better? After all of his snapping and grumbling? It was kinda working, though I would never tell him that. "I've done a lot more than that in heels and a ball gown," I said, and for the first time I heard how ridiculous a claim like that sounded. Especially considering I was pretty sure I'd said those very words before.

Seth cocked his head, squinting as he tried to figure me out. *Good luck.* "How does a princess like you know the capital of Laos?" he asked.

Though his question felt like it came out of nowhere, I shrugged. "Doesn't everyone?"

"Not the way I said it."

I rolled my eyes. "Are you trying to say you speak Lao on top of Turkish and Russian?"

He nearly choked on the spoonful of soup he'd just lifted to his mouth, and for a second he grasped his abdomen in pain as he coughed. "How the hell do you speak Turkish?" he gasped.

"I don't," I said with one eyebrow lifted.

"But you recognized it."

"So?"

Shaking his head, Seth slowly rose and returned to his couch. Apparently, though, our conversation wasn't finished: "Why did Geller leave you alive? No offense, but it would have been easier to kill you."

I took extreme offense to that, and if he could see my face he would have realized so. "Because I'm valuable," I said. *Obviously.*

Though I couldn't see him, I could hear the interest in his voice as he asked, "How valuable?"

My shields rose, leaving me wondering if I could really trust this stranger I was trapped with. Even if he was friends with Will, I didn't know Will enough to trust his friend. My situation wasn't much less dangerous than it had been in the warehouse, and I had to tread carefully.

"I'm not going to hurt you, Princess," Seth added, as if he knew my fears. "Who are you?"

Either my name would be dangerous, or it could keep me alive a bit longer, depending on how valuable I might be to someone like Seth. I wasn't anywhere close to home, and even Geller had only known my uncle, not me, so maybe I would be safe. But I wouldn't know if I didn't speak it out loud. "I'm Catherine Davenport," I said and tensed.

Seth actually sat up so he could look at me, his eyebrows high on his forehead as he took me in like he was seeing me for the first time. "Davenport," he said and locked eyes with me. "You're Milton's daughter, aren't you?"

And with that comment, my heart sank into my stomach. A soldier who had spent the last who knew how long on the other side of the world only had to hear my name to know exactly who I was, even if I was 3000 miles away from home. For the first time in my life, I didn't want to be well known. I wished I was normal and average so I could just go home and not have to wonder if everyone I met would be after my money and influence.

I was in trouble, and no matter how strong or smart I thought I was, I had no way to get myself out of it.

CHAPTER SIX

Seth was asleep. He hadn't lasted long after learning my name, though I was pretty sure he would have kept the conversation going if he'd had the energy. He knew who I was. He knew my dad, knew I was a long way from home, probably knew there'd be a hefty ransom on my head at this point. Seth was just a soldier, and I was pretty sure they weren't paid well. With the storm raging outside, I couldn't exactly go anywhere, and he knew it.

So he slept, and I washed dishes over and over again until my hands were raw, trying to come up with a plan to get myself to safety.

As soon as the storm stopped, I could run. I still had the map, and it would lead me down the mountain and hopefully to other people who could help me get in contact with the police. As long as I prepared ahead of time. There were some boots by the door, but I would need several pairs of socks to fit into them properly, and if I put on enough shirts and Will's thin jacket, I might stay warm enough. It wouldn't be easy, but it would work.

Ideally, Will would show up before I had to resort to wandering the frozen woods. He *was* the police, and cutting out the middleman would make things a lot smoother. I hated not knowing if I could fully trust him, though. What if he, like Seth, simply wanted to use me for the ransom? Dad probably hadn't answered his phone yet, so maybe that was why Will wasn't here yet. He was trying to get the right people to know I was even captured to make it worth his while.

"No," I muttered to myself. He wouldn't have sent me off into a blizzard if he wanted to use me to get money. It wasn't worth the risk when there was a chance I would get lost and freeze to death. No, he had to be on the good side. Seth, on the other hand…

I could see why Lanna didn't mind washing the dishes back at the Munroe Shack. Having something to do with my hands kept me from imagining my horrible demise. If I just kept busy, maybe I could keep away from Seth and his plans long enough to survive this place.

"NO!" Seth shouted suddenly.

The knife in my hand slipped, slicing my palm just beneath my thumb. I hissed with pain and grabbed a towel to soak up the blood, but Seth wasn't done screaming. I kept hold of the knife, just in case, and hurried around the counter expecting him to be fighting someone in the dim room.

He hadn't left the couch.

"Stop!" he growled, writhing where he lay and twisting himself up in the blankets as he fought nothing. "No. Don't—run! Let them go. Please—move in! Stop!" He was speaking nonsense, but the pain in his voice hit me hard. I set the knife on the end table before carefully approaching the couch.

He was dreaming. Or hallucinating. And he was going to hurt himself if he didn't stop fighting the blankets.

"Seth," I said warily, my heart pounding. "Seth, wake up."

"Please," he begged.

"Seth," I said louder, but I could barely hear myself as he started speaking orders to unseen people. "Seth!" I touched his shoulder.

He reacted immediately, grabbing my wrist and twisting me down. Pain shot through my arm as I fell, and I cried out as he rolled over and lifted his other arm to strike. Then he froze, staring down at me with wide eyes.

"Don't hurt me," I whispered, hot tears pooling in my eyes.

Seth pulled back, scrambling off of me and falling against the couch. And I ran. I grabbed the knife and dashed to the bedroom, locking the door behind me.

"Catherine!" Seth shouted after me. His voice barely made it through the door, but I could hear his footsteps shuffling closer.

I pressed myself into the corner of the room, behind the bed with my knife held tight.

"Catherine, I'm sorry."

My palm was still bleeding, soaking through the towel and aching sharply. And while I could barely see through my tears, I kept my eyes locked on the door.

"I didn't mean… Catherine, just let me explain."

"Stay away from me." He could have killed me. In his sleep, no less. My whole arm ached as I huddled in my hiding place, every inch of me tense. He could have killed me.

"I'm so sorry," he said one more time, and then his footsteps retreated back to the front room.

I broke. For the first time since arriving at this stupid cabin, I sobbed without trying to hold it back. I didn't have the strength to keep it in anymore, and I sobbed until I was absolutely exhausted and couldn't stay awake.

* * *

Waking up to the sight of a bloody hand towel and a wickedly sharp knife only inches from my face was not high on my list of favorite things. Neither was the headache that came with my return to consciousness, or the ache in my chest that came from knowing my troubles were far from over. Worst of all was waking up to a gentle knock on the door and a voice I had absolutely no desire to hear.

"Catherine? Are you awake?"

"No," I replied.

"Well, then I hope you enjoy sleeping."

He had no right to sound annoyed. The man had attacked me, and he thought he could take that tone with me? In my normal life, no man would have gotten away with sounding like I was making his life difficult, and this cabin and the soldier inside it were far from resembling anything normal.

"Just leave me alone," I said.

"I'm pretty sure it's freezing in there," he replied.

Almost on cue, a shiver ran through me. Most of the blankets were out in the front room where I'd left them as we ate, and the warmth of the fire definitely didn't penetrate a closed door. Still, I wasn't going to leave this room for anything. "I can handle a little cold," I said, though my voice shook when I shivered. "Go back to your corner of the cabin."

"I'll make some bacon," he tried next.

My stomach growled in response. "I'm not hungry."

"And I got the radio working."

I didn't need music. I needed to go home. "I don't care about—"

"Will's on the other end."

Before I consciously realized what he said, I leapt up and pulled the door open with barely guarded hope that he wasn't lying to me.

Seth leaned against the wall opposite the door, keeping his distance and his eyes focused on the spot just above my head. The coward couldn't even look me in the eye. "Will has an old ham radio," he explained, keeping his voice impressively soft. "I turned it on hoping to find information about the storm, and instead I found—"

"Will," I gasped. I had no idea how much relief I could feel just knowing he was on the other side of a radio. It felt like the whole cabin had warmed up, and I didn't even mourn the fact that I'd left the knife on the far side of the bedroom. "I want to talk to him."

Nodding once, Seth led the way to the table where he'd set the old-looking box. "Don't say anything about where you are," he instructed as he held a headset out to me. "Just in case."

I was so eager to have any sort of connection to the outside world that I agreed without hesitation. Will knew where I was, anyway. "Will?" I whispered into the headset, and suddenly I was afraid he wasn't there when I got no immediate response. What if Seth just used the radio to lure me out?

Seth reached over to the far edge of the unit and tapped a few times with a metal piece. Morse code, I realized. Long short long short. Short long. Long. *C. A. T.*

"Catherine?" Will's voice crackled through the headphones, but I recognized it easily. "Catherine are you okay? Thank God you made it." I could barely hear him, but that didn't make his words any less comforting. And if he'd been talking to Seth, he must not have been worried about his friend being here, which made me feel just a little bit better about the soldier standing next to me. But only a little.

"I'm okay," I replied, doing my best to speak clearly. Not easy, with Seth's scowl hovering nearby. "What's going on? What's happening with Geller?"

The first half of his reply got lost in static, and I only caught, "word...you safe as soon as I can." It was not reassuring.

"Will, I want to go home."

"I know. And you will. But until I can..." Until he could what? What was he trying to say that the radio wouldn't let him?

Seth must have sensed my distress, because he returned to his Morse code. I couldn't understand all of the letters he tapped, but I figured the gist of it when he sent 'no sound' and settled in the chair. That was all the talking I was going to get.

Several beeps answered his message, and I stared at Seth, hoping he would translate for me.

He coughed, giving me a glance, then muttered, "He says 'stay strong.'" Seth's answer was a lot longer, and I caught the words 'too long,' 'girl,' and 'crazy.'

I narrowed my eyes, but Seth was focused on his tapped conversation.

Will said something about a job.

Seth tapped the words 'not safe.'

'Safe,' Will replied, along with that shortened version of my name again.

"Don't be a hero, William Dunn," Seth growled under his breath.

Fear trickled back into me, stiffening my spine as I sat there trying my best to remember the letters as Will's response came through. He was saying G had a plan. Geller, probably. And that plan involved money. My money, most likely. Had Dad answered the ransom call? Or was the problem that he hadn't?

"That doesn't fit," Seth mumbled, looking at the radio as if it had all the answers. "He'd need someone more influential than rich if that's what you're thinking." 'Power,' he tapped. 'Not money.'

'Hastings,' Will replied.

Seth swore, growing pale. Grabbing the headset from me, he said, "Get far away," before tapping the same thing in code, and then he switched the radio off.

"Wait," I protested, staring at the silver box and feeling what little hope I had fizzle into nothing. "But I didn't get to…" *Do anything.* I'd barely said two sentences to him.

But Seth shook his head, his eyes unfocused as he sat there. "Too dangerous," he said, his voice rough, and he rose to head back to his couch.

I was not about to let him dictate my every moment here in this awful cabin. "That doesn't get to be your decision," I said.

He ignored me.

"You can't just walk away from me," I said next, but that didn't work either. "Who the hell is Hastings?"

Seth froze, suddenly rigid as he stood in front of the glowing fire.

"And what does he have to do with Geller?" I added warily. If I needed them, there were more knives in the kitchen, though Seth would probably cut me off before I could get to them. I had to be careful. Just because he had sort of let me talk to Will, it didn't mean I could trust the half-dead soldier.

Seth turned his head only enough to look at me from the corner of his eye. "You are full of surprises, aren't you, Miss Davenport?" The way he spoke, with arrogance coloring his words, sounded familiar. Not his voice specifically, just the way he formed his words. With a slight drawl and a confidence that gave his words strength. I'd heard my name said that way so many times that hearing it now almost made me feel a little more at home.

"Who stabbed you, Seth?" I asked, and I had a feeling he might actually answer me this time.

He turned his head a little more and said, "I never knew his name."

"But he was American," I guessed. "Dark hair, five foot nine, a cleft in his chin?"

Seth's fingers curled into fists.

"Power, not money," I continued as a piece of the Seth puzzle—and my own puzzle—slowly fell into place. Geller was searching for something in the area, something he thought was important enough to stay close to the place he'd stolen a painting worth millions, a place where he was more likely to get caught. "Hastings," I whispered. I knew that name. More importantly, I knew that name in a position of importance. Power, specifically.

What had Will said about Geller? *There's nothing Geller likes more than targeting a government official.*

"The Secretary of Homeland Security," Seth said, guessing at my thoughts.

I'd met the man once or twice during my couple semesters of school in D.C. Spending my sophomore year that far from home hadn't been my favorite time, but it was where I learned how to fit in with the part of higher society that valued position over wealth. Secretary Hastings, handsome and charming to boot, had succumbed to my own charms like many others and told me all about his son while treating me to a dinner cruise on the Potomac. A son, he'd said, who was knee deep in the Army.

"Seth Hastings," I said, staring at his back and trying to understand how I hadn't put it together sooner. He looked a lot like his dad, the same sandy hair and the strikingly turquoise eyes. But if Seth really was a Hastings, that meant he came from one of the wealthiest families on the East Coast. He was one of my kind.

"Best not to say my name out loud," Seth muttered.

"Geller is looking for you," I replied. "That's why he didn't run with the painting he stole."

Slowly sinking onto the couch, Seth actually looked a little worried as he stared at the kitchen wall, his gaze a little unfocused. "I'd hoped…" he muttered then closed his eyes. If a hulking man like Seth Hastings, who could buy his way out of any problem his physique couldn't solve, was nervous, that didn't make me feel any better. At all.

Desperate for a change in subject, I looked out the windows that were nearly completely covered in snow. "Has the storm stopped even a little?"

Seth shook his head, following my gaze. "I've never seen anything like it," he said. "At least it means no one can get up this far. For now."

So we were safe. Sort of. Suddenly my blanket didn't seem all that adequate, and I shuffled a little closer to the fire. Our wood pile was running low, but I wasn't sure I had the strength to go out and get more. Not with the snow pelting the cabin and my thoughts spinning and my heart racing with a fear I couldn't seem to control. If Geller was after Seth, for whatever reason, that meant he would probably be trying a lot harder than if he'd only been looking for me. I was not nearly as big a prize as the man on the couch.

I needed something to distract me. Something good. And while my usual distractions required another person, I wasn't about to suggest that idea to Seth. He was the last person I would want to join in on that.

"This reminds me of Switzerland," I said, not sure why I did. Grabbing a chair from the table, I set it near the fireplace and watched the flames instead of looking at Seth, though I could feel his eyes on me. "I was eight years old, and a storm like this came out of nowhere when we were visiting Davos."

"Davos," Seth repeated, and he sounded surprised. "Who in their right mind chooses to visit Davos?"

I turned to glare at him, but he only raised an eyebrow. "Mom chose," I said. "Dad wanted to stay in Lucerne, but Mom wanted to see the smaller cities. But when the snow came, we were trapped for almost a week. Dad was furious that no amount of money could get us out of there, though he definitely tried. Mom turned it into a game. She said we were bears, and it was time to hibernate for winter. Mama Bear and her cub. We built a giant blanket fort, gathered a bunch of snacks, and we didn't leave the parlor for two days. Dad was furious, but Mom didn't care." A tear slipped down my cheek, coming out of nowhere. Hadn't I cried enough already? But I hadn't talked about Switzerland in I couldn't remember how long, and I wasn't even sure if I'd ever told anyone about one of my favorite memories.

No one would have cared about a story like that.

"She died less than a year later," I said and stared into the fire. If I had known I wouldn't have my mom for much longer, I would have prayed for a million snowstorms just to have more happy memories like that. The decade since then hadn't had many.

"I dream about the war," Seth said quietly, but he wasn't looking at me. His eyes glittered in the firelight, and I couldn't quite figure out what his expression meant. "Every time I close my eyes, it's like I'm right in the middle of it."

I looked back at him, wondering if I even wanted to know what he saw when he slept. With the way it made him tremble now and scream before, a man who had no reason to be afraid of anything, I wasn't sure I could handle hearing about it. Not on top of everything else.

Seth still didn't meet my gaze but stared up at the dark ceiling now. "I wish we could choose what we remember," he continued, and I breathed a sigh of relief. "I'd rather have a memory like yours than what I see."

I'd heard the man laugh once since I met him, and I wasn't sure he'd ever really smiled. Did he have *anything* happy to think about? Just as I was about to ask—though I wasn't sure why I cared—my stomach rumbled loudly.

As he glanced over, the corner of Seth's mouth twitched. "I promised you bacon, didn't I?" he said and sat up.

That sounded amazing. "You did," I agreed, grateful for the lighter topic. "I hope that wasn't a lie to get me out here."

"A bribe," he corrected. "Not a lie." But as soon as he stood, he swayed on his feet and collapsed back onto the couch with his face shining a frightening white. He shut his eyes tight, hand over his waist, and seemed to be holding his breath as he waited for the pain to subside.

Well that wasn't much help. "Tell me what to do," I grumbled as I draped my blanket over the back of the chair. At least I'd be able to surprise Lanna with newfound cooking skills if I got back. When. *When* I got back. There was no point in being pessimistic.

"No," Seth replied and tried to get back up. He failed miserably, his whole body shaking. "No, I should..."

If I'd thought he could actually stand, I would have pushed him back onto the couch. But I just stood there and watched his pathetic attempt. "Seth," I said after giving him a few seconds to try. "You're basically useless. Just tell me what to do, and I promise I won't burn the bacon."

As he lay back down, I thought I heard him grumble something that sounded like, "Don't make promises you can't keep." But he looked at me with resignation and sighed, "Fine. First you have to take care of your hand."

"My..." I stared at my left hand. Somehow I'd completely forgotten about the slice through the bottom of my palm, though the ache had never really left. It had just blended in with the other aches in my body. "Oh."

"What happened?"

You screamed and scared me out of my mind. But for some reason I didn't want to make him feel worse, so I shrugged. "I accidentally cut myself."

"Is it deep?"

Why did he care? It was his own fault, yeah, but he didn't have to make a big deal out of it. "Maybe," I said, trying to decide if I couldn't move my thumb because of the pain or because I'd really cut deep enough to do some damage. As soon as I cleaned it, I'd be able to tell better, but that would be painful. I wasn't sure I had the energy to deal with that just yet.

"Catherine," Seth growled. "Let me look at it."

"It's fine," I assured him. That would mean I had to get close enough for him to touch me, and I wasn't ready for that yet. Or ever.

Seth tried to sit up again but couldn't do it.

"Stop that," I warned him. "You'll tear your stitches or something, and I don't want to have to do them again."

"*You* might need stitches," he countered.

Probably. "I'm fine," I said again.

He literally growled in annoyance. "Why are you so goddamn stubborn?"

"You must be rubbing off on me," I replied and moved for the kitchen. "Where's the bacon?"

"Catherine."

"Do you want to eat or not?" Ah, the precooked meat thing in the cupboard was apparently bacon. Not exactly what I hoped for, but it was better than nothing. Was I supposed to eat it cold, or could I warm it up somehow?

"Forget about the food, Catherine," Seth said, and I could hear him struggling again.

"Don't you dare get off that couch," I snapped. "You're going to get yourself killed for real."

"Not if you drive me insane first," he growled back.

I decided to put the dry strips of meat onto a frying pan, though I made sure not to turn it all the way to high this time. It wasn't exactly the way our chef cooked bacon, since he always worked with the finest raw cuts, but I could try to mimic what he did and hope for the best.

"Don't keep it on one side for too long."

I couldn't help but smile in triumph. Dad always told me I was the most stubborn thing he'd ever met, and I tried to live up to that declaration as often as I could because it annoyed him. Who would have thought, though, that my determination would lead to me actually cooking my own bacon in the middle of a snowstorm, listening to grumbled instructions from a half-dead soldier?

* * *

When nighttime rolled around—though I hardly noticed a change in the darkness outside—I could barely handle the pain in my hand. I could bite back a lot when required, but I'd never been good with pain, and considering I didn't have much else to think about with Seth unconscious on the couch, I was ready to break down.

Rinsing the blood from my palm had been bad enough, the water stinging every time it moved a bit of raw skin. I'd wrapped a clean towel around it while I cooked the bacon, but an hour after our little dinner, I was reduced to tears again.

I had to do something about the cut. Leaving it barely clean would only lead to infection, and while it wasn't as bad as the hole in Seth's stomach, it would probably start to cause some problems. But the aching pain I endured as I sat on the bed was nothing compared to the fire that would come as soon as I worked up enough courage to clean it out and see just how bad it was.

Mom would have known how to make the pain easier to deal with. She wasn't stupid enough to lie and tell me it wouldn't be there, but she would have thought of a fun game to keep my mind off of things. When I burned my hand when I was four, she'd spent the night telling me stories of princes and dragons and princesses saving the day so I wouldn't think about the never-ending heat that came with the injury.

I'd barely thought about Mom over the years, but something about this cabin brought memories of her closer to the surface. I didn't like it.

I moaned a little, gripping my left wrist tightly and clenching my jaw. What I wouldn't give to be unconscious right now. Seth probably hadn't felt a thing while I redid the stitches on his stomach, though I didn't envy the pain that would follow him for a while.

Another whimper came out of me as pain shot through my hand. *Enough stalling.* I had to deal with it sooner or later. I had little hope of getting to any sort of doctor, not with the way the wind howled outside. This problem, like so many others, was one I had to fix on my own.

"Are you going to let me help you now?" Seth asked from the doorway.

I looked up even as I tightened my grip on my wrist. "I'm fine," I said, wondering how many times I had said that lie over the years.

His scowl sent a wave of fear through me that made me feel ridiculous. But I had legitimately feared for my life when I tried to wake him from his dream, and he looked terrifying with that anger in his eyes. "I've dealt with difficult soldiers before," he said. "Either you choose to let me help you with your hand, or I will force you to let me. It's up to you."

I didn't doubt he could make good on that threat. Glancing at the knife I'd left on the foot of the bed and wondering if I needed to keep it with me, I took a fortifying breath. He was still injured, I reminded myself, and probably not as strong as he usually was. If I had to, I could fight him off.

While Seth retrieved the sewing kit I'd used and cleaned the needle with vodka, I sat at the table and soaked my hand in a bowl of warm water, both annoyed that I hadn't thought to do that myself and grateful that Seth had thought of a gentler way to clean the cut than running water over it. While it still stung horribly, it certainly could have been worse.

"This'll be the hard part," Seth said as he sat next to me. "One of the hard parts," he amended and added a sympathetic grimace. He held the vodka in one hand and had the other stretched out toward me, waiting for me to give him my hand.

I was strong. I could do this.

Slowly lifting my hand out of the water, I let it drip dry for a second then rested it in his large palm. His hands were huge, making mine look tiny by comparison. Everything about the man was huge, from his height to his shoulders to the way he seemed to fill the room just with his presence. I'd met a few elites who could do that, but Seth's presence was less from his social standing and more from the strength he seemed to exude just by leading the life he had.

Why would he choose the dangerous life of a soldier overseas when he could live in absolute luxury and never have to worry about a thing?

Just as Seth was about to pour the alcohol over my palm, I snatched it from him and quickly swallowed the biggest mouthful I could handle, hoping it would hit me quickly and help numb the pain. Seth just stared at me, both impressed and alarmed by how easily I swallowed the burning alcohol. I got that reaction a lot.

I also got his following question a lot: "How old are you, Catherine?"

Employing my usual technique, I gave him a smile and asked, "How old do you think I am?" The answers to that usually ranged from twenty-one to twenty-six, a fact I was quite proud of.

But Seth shook his head, furrowing his eyebrows as he carefully examined my face. "That's not an answer to my question."

I realized I'd cried off all my makeup. My hair was an absolute mess. Without my own clothes, I had no way to accentuate my figure. More likely than not, I actually looked my age for the first time in years. Deflating quickly, I turned my gaze to the rough wood grain of the table and muttered, "Eighteen." *Barely.* And even if I couldn't see his face, I could feel his disapproval. Most men were impressed by how old I could act. Seth, apparently, was not.

Sudden sharp pain shot through my hand, so intense that I shrieked and drew my hand back, dripping with vodka. His lips tight, Seth just grabbed the needle and pulled a length of thread through it. "Sorry," he said, sounding completely unrepentant. "It's easier when you're not anticipating it."

I grumbled a few words at him that made his eyes grow wider.

"Wow," he said, though I didn't think he was impressed at all by my more colorful vocabulary. "I rarely hear that even with my soldiers."

I reluctantly placed my hand back in his, my eyes on the needle he held. "Why did you choose the Army?" I asked. Talking would at least distract me a little.

A hint of a smile flashed across Seth's lips but didn't linger. "I figured my dad would hate it more than anything else I chose."

"But he's Homeland Security," I countered. "Wouldn't he be proud to—Ouch!"

Seth gripped my wrist before I could pull my hand away and tear through the hole he'd just put in my skin. "If I went into politics like him, maybe he would be proud," he said. "But I went into basic training, starting at the bottom like everyone else. He hated that."

That made sense. With a name like Hastings, Seth was probably expected to stay high in the social ranks. If I had any brothers, Dad would have been mortified if they did anything remotely common. "Do you have siblings?" I asked.

Completing his first stitch, Seth shook his head and cleaned the needle on a vodka-soaked towel. "I am the only Hastings. You?"

"No." It had been hard enough to get me, and Mom had cried more than once when she realized she couldn't have any more kids. And Dad had done his very best to make sure he didn't produce any other nuisances with his other wives. As he'd told me many times, he couldn't fathom having to deal with anyone else on top of me.

"Maybe your dad worried about who would keep the Hastings name going if you were killed," I said. My own dad had mourned more than once that my cousin Matthew was the only one who would keep the Davenport name. Maybe if he knew Matthew wasn't the disappointment he thought he was, he wouldn't be so cold to Lanna's family.

Seth smiled a little and poked the needle into my skin once more. Man, that hurt, and I took another quick swig of vodka. "Trust me," he said quietly, "the Hastings name is better off without me."

I wasn't sure what to say to that, so I kept my mouth shut and focused on not cursing from pain. It was becoming increasingly difficult, even with the vodka. He'd only done two stitches, and I probably needed at least three more.

"You don't have to avoid the front room, you know," Seth said after a while. "It's warmer out here, and I don't bite."

If he hadn't been holding on so tight, I would have torn my hand out of his grip. If he stabbed me so deep one more time… "I'm not sure I can believe that," I said, barely keeping myself from gritting my teeth and being unintelligible. "This is definitely your fault."

He froze just before poking the needle into my skin again. "What?"

I'd decided against saying anything, since it would only make things more tense, but the pain was clouding my judgment. Or maybe that was the vodka. "You scared me," I admitted. "My hand slipped." Honestly, cutting my hand wasn't nearly the worst of that moment. If I thought too hard, I could quite clearly picture how close to really hurting me Seth had come. I was a long way from trusting he wouldn't do that again if I gave him the chance.

"Catherine," Seth said.

I knew he was looking at me, but I kept my eyes on my sliced thumb. "I'm—"

"Fine," he finished, and the annoyance in the word made me flinch and try once more to pull my hand away. "Catherine, you don't have to be fine. I'm sorry about your hand. And for…" How clearly did he remember that moment I tried to wake him up? "It's worse when I'm injured," he tried to explain. "Harder to control. But I've never had it this bad before. I couldn't… It's like I get stuck in the same ten-second loop, and no matter how hard I try, I can't change anything. I couldn't pull myself out of it this time."

That made me look up. "How often do you get hurt?" I asked, though I knew there was more to it than that. I couldn't really focus any deeper than that with my head spinning just a bit.

He almost laughed. "You mean how often do I not?" he amended.

I could see a scar near his right ear, cutting across his cheekbone and into his sideburn. I'd noticed a couple others near the wound I stitched for him, not to mention his more recent injuries that were probably more than just superficial. I knew being a soldier was dangerous, but something in the way Seth said it felt different. "What were you doing in Laos?" I whispered.

Seth's hand slipped, sticking the needle straight into my palm. He cursed and pulled both his hands away, pressing one to his forehead. Before he tucked the other under the table, I saw it tremoring. "Sorry," he said and took several deep breaths, his eyes shut.

"Seth," I pressed. Something told me he needed to talk about it, or his dreams would only get worse. Besides, the fact that he immediately pulled away after hurting me made me want to think maybe I could trust him. He didn't want to hurt me. Reaching out, I gently touched his arm until he looked at me with his vivid eyes. "Seth, it's okay. I shouldn't have sprung the question on you."

For the first time since meeting him, there was nothing about him that was frightening as he looked at me and tried to read my expression. "Special Forces," he said after nearly a minute of silence. "There was a…" Picking up the needle, he cleaned it again and reached out for my hand. But he stopped halfway, staring at his own fingers as they shook. "Hostage situation," he whispered without looking away from his tremoring hand.

Let them go, he'd said in his nightmare. Fear crept into my chest, my heart beating quickly as I fought against imagining what that would feel like. I only ever cared for myself. If I were responsible for someone else, I'd fall to pieces because I was hard enough to deal with on my own. But the worst part as I sat there was wondering if his mission had been successful. Had he managed to get the hostages to safety, or…?

"Hostiles took an American family," Seth said quietly, and his eyes grew darker. "Hoping to draw my unit out. They knew we were there escorting the US Ambassador, but they shouldn't have known. No one should have known. The family were civilians. Innocents."

A shudder ran through him, and I took his hand to keep it from shaking. Though the motion felt strange to me, it seemed to give Seth a little strength, though I wondered if he was actually aware of my touch. He was pretty lost in his story as he spoke.

"Half my unit was dead before we even breached the building," he said, his voice growing lower. "The rest barely made it inside. My partner was shot down right in front of me. And when I tried to return fire, the hostiles used the family as shields. I couldn't… They took me. Tied me up. But they didn't kill me. Why wouldn't they kill me?" His eyebrows pulled together, and suddenly he returned my grip on his hand, squeezing so tight it hurt. "They should have killed me like the rest," he said.

I tried to pull my hand away, but he held fast. "Seth," I said. "Seth, let go of me."

"They used the family to lure me in, but I couldn't give them what they wanted. They should have killed me."

"Seth!" I tugged as hard as I could. Pain shot through my wrist and shoulder, but my fingers slipped free as I fell back against my chair and hit my elbow on the wood with a bang. Almost instantly Seth shouted, "Get down!" and tackled me. As we hit the ground hard, Seth's full weight on top of me, the wind was knocked out of me, and I let out a cry of pain.

The instant Seth rolled away, I curled up in a protective ball and waited for him to attack. But he didn't. And when I looked up, he was already on the other side of the room, staring at me with watery eyes and so much fear in his face.

"Catherine," he whispered and took a single step toward me.

"Don't," I said, barely managing to get the word out. Stumbling to my feet, I carefully made my way across the room as his eyes followed me. He took another step, and I couldn't stop myself from flinching. "Stay away from me," I begged, even though I knew he hadn't been trying to hurt me. He'd probably even been protecting me. But that didn't make him and his sheer size and strength any less frightening, so as soon as I reached the hallway, I ran for the bedroom and locked it behind me before sinking into the corner behind the bed, hiding once again.

I had my own fears and insecurities to deal with.

I wasn't sure I could handle his too.

CHAPTER SEVEN

Eventually I fell asleep, when my vigilant watch lasted long enough that I was too exhausted to keep my eyes open. Though I never heard a single sound from Seth, I knew he was just on the other side of the wall, maybe even at the door, waiting to apologize and try to explain. I didn't want to pity the poor soldier who had been through trauma. I wanted to go home.

I just wanted to go home.

My restless sleep, still wedged in the corner, did more harm than good. I kept dreaming about Seth's face. The pain that triggered him to action. What if he slipped too far into his own nightmare that he couldn't come back out again? What would I do then?

I dreamed I was in a rundown shack in Vientiane, Matthew and Lanna and Adam next to me. Men held us at gunpoint, and machine guns and cries of pain echoed around the building, slowly drawing closer and closer. One soldier made it in, and he froze in the doorway, his vivid blue eyes wide and helpless as he stared at us. He held his gun, but he knew he couldn't use it, and he locked eyes with me, his expression full of desperation.

Take me and let them go, he said, holding up his hands in surrender.

The gunmen grabbed him and led him away, and one of them laughed and came to crouch in front of me. The face of Max Geller greeted me, and he reached out and stroked my cheek. *Don't worry*, he told me. *We'll take very good care of him.*

The sounds of Seth screaming in pain woke me up, and I wasn't sure if it was in the dream or real life.

Not that it mattered, because I had no intention of going into that front room unless I absolutely had to.

* * *

A shower did me a world of good, though I couldn't totally wash away the tension that had built up in my shoulders the last couple of days. My heart didn't seem to want to slow down to a normal pace, either, and my head ached from my dreams and fitful sleep, Still, it was nice to let the warm water run over me and help me forget, if only for a moment, that I had no way to better my situation. No amount of charm or smiles or even money could get me back home. Not yet.

I combed my fingers through my hair as I stepped out of the shower, but I didn't let myself look in the mirror. I was afraid of what I would find, and I knew I had no way to fix it. Who did I have to impress, anyway? Just Seth, and the young soldier was far too broken to be setting his sights anywhere but himself.

Taking that shower had given me some clarity when it came to Seth, and being away from him for a while had probably helped too. He really hadn't been trying to hurt me, so could I really blame him for trying to protect me, even if the threat wasn't real? Eventually I would have to apologize for the way I reacted, but I wasn't quite ready for that.

No matter how bad I felt for probably making his emotional pain worse, that wouldn't be an easy conversation.

So after I got dressed, I sat on the lid of the toilet and grabbed the magazine sitting behind it, knowing I couldn't hide forever but wanting to all the same.

The tabloid didn't exactly seem like something Will would read, but what did I know about the cop? I'd spent all of twenty minutes with him at most, and I wasn't entirely sure I even remembered what he looked like. If he showed up here with a crowd of people, I probably couldn't have picked him out. Maybe he enjoyed reading about the rich and famous. Maybe he only had four toes on his right foot. Maybe he wasn't a cop at all and was trying to get his own ransom.

"Stop thinking that," I scolded myself quietly and returned my focus to the magazine.

Another celebrity had ended up in rehab. *Big surprise there.* Pixie cuts were the new thing, though I would never in a million years try that hairstyle and get rid of the waves my mom had always loved. Apparently the best way to lose weight was to eat nothing but broccoli, which was nothing short of ridiculous. With every story I read, I felt a little more like the world in which I lived was just as silly and frivolous as those reality TV shows I loved, and I could hardly stomach the thought enough to keep reading.

When I turned the next page, I gasped.

Seth Hastings: The Man, The Myth, The Legend.

No way. There was a story about Seth. I knew he was from a famous family, but I had no idea he was big enough to have an entire three-page story in one of the country's top tabloids. How had I never paid attention to him before now? If I had seen him as he was in the full page photo sitting beneath the headline—dazzling smile, extremely well dressed, eyes full of life and laughter—I probably would have crossed the country just to find him. I'd certainly done just that for many others, none of them nearly as handsome as "the nation's golden hero," as the article termed him.

"Who are you, Seth Hastings?" I whispered and dove in, desperate to get any insight to the ridiculously large man on the other side of the door.

Seth was born in Napa Valley, in the midst of all the vineyards and wealth that came with them. Thalia Hastings was an heiress to one of the largest wineries in the state, and Gordon Hastings had been in politics since the day he retired from an extensive career in the military. *Interesting.* Seth grew up in California until his father was appointed to an undisclosed position in Washington D.C., where the family moved when Seth was fifteen. The family were often seen among the elite in the country's capital city, and Seth quickly became a heartthrob once he enrolled at Yale. He even did a bit of modeling—*see page 78*, where a younger Seth's face advertised up close and personal a fancy watch that had been squeezed into the corner.

After finishing college and getting a degree in Economics, Seth enrolled in the military and rose through the ranks at an alarming speed. The author of the article apparently followed him to Iraq and had many thrilling things to say about his heroism overseas and how they always came out victorious if Seth was there. I skipped over that part mostly, not really caring to revisit my last encounter with the soldier. What I *was* interested in was the last section, the one talking about the woman he left behind.

According to the picture, which showed Seth and a golden-haired beauty walking arm in arm down a street as if on a casual shopping trip, Seth had been head over heels in love. The way he looked at her even as she smiled at something across the street, it was like he'd never been happier to be with another person in his life. Lissa Montgomery, whom he'd met at Yale, was a picture of perfection, and the author of the article couldn't seem to stop praising her grace and class and social prowess, though she came from humble circumstances. Everything I aspired to be, she came across naturally. Supposedly they were still together, and the author hinted at a wedding of royal proportions in the near future.

If Seth looked at her like that when they were just walking down the street, why did he come to a friend's cabin instead of going home? Had he gone insane? And why wasn't this Lissa doing a full-blown manhunt for her almost fiancé? If I were in her position, I didn't think I would have even let him go in the first place. Not when he was—I glanced down at the article—"A gentleman of the highest order and America's saving grace."

Curiosity and anger overpowered the last of my fear, and I stepped out of the bathroom with the magazine in tow, ready to tell Seth that as soon as the snow stopped, he had to go straight back to Connecticut and end the girl's misery. But as I got to the front room, I stopped dead, staring at the couch.

Seth wasn't there.

He wasn't anywhere. Not in the kitchen, or the bedroom, or lurking in any dark corner of the house. The wind was still howling, but maybe the snow had lessened while I showered. My heart actually sank as I considered the possibility that Seth had decided to leave me here on my own to fend for myself. He'd probably think it was safer for me, given his behavior the last couple of days, but that didn't make me feel any better. I wasn't sure how long I could actually last by myself, no matter how many times I told myself I was strong and could handle anything.

That lie didn't sound as convincing as it used to.

The front door burst open with a flurry of snow, and fear shot through me followed quickly by relief. "You're still here," I said as soon as I could breathe again.

Seth raised an eyebrow before setting his armful of wood next to the fireplace. "Am I not supposed to be?" he asked, and though he tried for a teasing tone, his question was real. Snow clung to his sandy hair, and red painted his cheeks with color I hadn't seen in his face until now, and I suddenly found myself feeling just a little jealous of perfect Lissa Montgomery. Seth was undeniably attractive.

"Look," he said when I didn't answer, and I could tell he was trying really hard to keep his voice soft. "I have no right to expect you to forgive me, but I'm sorry. I didn't mean to hurt you, and I shouldn't have been talking about Laos in the first place. The less you know about me, the better."

I had a whole magazine sitting on a side table next to me that told me a lot more than I wanted to know. "Why didn't you go to a hospital, Seth?" I asked, and he furrowed his brow in confusion. "Why would you come here, where there was no one to help you?"

Brushing a bit of snow from his shoulder, he watched me carefully, probably trying to decide if he even wanted to answer my question. But then he sighed. "Partly because I didn't want them to find me," he said softly.

"Who? The men who captured you?"

Seth paled a little, fear leaking out in his expression, but then he shook his head. "It wouldn't be the end of the world if Geller found me again."

I could have argued, but I kept my mouth shut.

"My father," he continued. "The press. Anyone. I didn't want anyone to know I was home."

"But why?" I pushed.

Sadness suddenly overwhelmed his features, and Seth folded his arms as he stood there and muttered, "Because they would call me a hero."

He looked so heartbroken that I was afraid to keep asking questions, but my curiosity was winning. "Aren't you?" I asked quietly. Silently, I added, *What happened to the family you were trying to save?*

Tears pooled in his vivid eyes, and an ache settled in my chest as I watched him try to hold himself together. He wasn't doing a very good job. He didn't have to say anything to tell me that he'd failed his mission, and it was eating him alive.

No wonder he couldn't sleep.

"Seth," I whispered.

He coughed and slipped his trembling hands into his pockets as his body went a little rigid. "I need to talk about something else," he said, and his voice tremored too.

A wave of dizziness passed over me as I realized how close he was to slipping into another episode, which I did not under any circumstances want to witness. "Right," I said, and I glanced at the magazine next to me. Maybe not that. I searched the rest of the cabin for something—anything—we could talk about, and my eyes landed on a stack of old games in the corner by the table. "How are you at chess?"

Following my gaze, Seth smiled just a little. "I'm really good at chess," he replied.

"Probably not as good as me."

"Is that a challenge?"

I hurried over and grabbed the dusty box, setting it down on the table as Seth took a seat opposite me with a bit of excitement in those turquoise eyes of his. "It's absolutely a challenge," I said, "unless you're afraid you'll lose."

His expression turned into a smug grin that temporarily distracted me as I was opening the box. Goodness, no wonder he had done some modeling. "I never lose," he said.

I coughed and shook my head a little, trying to clear my thoughts. "Well," I said, "I always win, so this is going to be interesting."

There were a few missing pieces once we'd managed to set up the board. On top of a few pawns, Seth's black queen was nowhere to be found, and my white knight had vanished at some point over the years. Both of us looked around for things we could use in place of the missing parts, and by the time we'd filled in the pawns with dry conchiglie pasta for me and bits of wood for Seth, he grabbed a saltshaker and put it where his queen should be.

"No way," I said and put it where my knight belonged. Then I unclasped one of my earrings and set it in place of his queen. "The queen is the most powerful piece, so you can't have a saltshaker be your queen."

"And why does your earring get to be so special?" he asked.

"This thing cost me five hundred bucks."

He rolled his eyes. "And you don't think my saltshaker is valuable?"

"It's a saltshaker, Seth. Can we just play already?" I moved a pawn forward.

"Fine," he said and pushed one of his wood pawns forward two spaces. "As long as you're ready to lose."

I gave him my best smug smile to let him know I couldn't be intimidated so easily. Chess was one thing I knew I was good at, and I highly doubted a soldier had the skills to challenge me. This was going to be fun.

Five minutes into the game, which so far had been going exactly as I hoped, Seth struck up conversation. "So how does a princess like you know how to play so well? Are chess clubs cool now?"

I gazed at him while he considered his move, and I wondered just how old he actually was. His size made him seem older, but when he was relaxed like this he didn't seem to have too many years on me. Based on that magazine article, he had done at least a few years of military service after getting his four-year degree, so he had to be at least twenty-five. But beyond that, I had no idea.

He glanced up at me then laughed a little. "I'm twenty-six," he said. "That's what you're wondering, right?"

"How did—"

"Chess clubs probably aren't even a thing anymore, are they?" He moved his rook forward and took out one of my pasta shell pawns.

"Honestly, I have no idea," I said. "I'm always too busy to pay attention to stuff like that." I moved my bishop a few squares diagonally forward.

Seth captured my bishop with his knight without hesitation then said, "What keeps you so busy? Shopping trips and days at the spa?"

Only sometimes. I shouldn't have felt so offended by his comment, but I was. There was so much more to me than a spoiled little rich kid, but no one seemed to get past that part. "Do you really think so little of me?" I asked, growling the words a little.

"It's your turn."

I captured his knight with my saltshaker. "I'm not some entitled brat who thinks she's better than everyone," I said. "You don't know anything about me."

Unperturbed by my raised voice, Seth kept his eyes on the game and moved one of his pawns. "True, I've only known you a couple days," he said, "but you're really not that hard to figure out. You grew up with plenty of money—"

"So did you," I pointed out.

He ignored me. "But you went to all those fancy schools where everyone else has money too, so you had to find more and more ways to stand out and be special because you've been told all your life you're special. And when something doesn't go your way, you expect everyone else to fix it for you because that's how it's always been. It's your turn."

I shifted my other bishop then scowled at him. "You're not that hard to figure out either," I said. "Born to riches and fame, you couldn't handle the pressure and ran away to the other side of the world to get away from it. But you can't change who you are, so now you're probably even more famous than before, and you must hate that."

Seth rolled his eyes. "Do you ever get tired of pretending you're so high and mighty? Check."

I reluctantly moved my king out of danger. "Do you ever get tired of being a giant?" I retorted, though it wasn't my best comeback, since I was trying to focus on the game and figure out how to win. Suddenly he was making it difficult. "How tall are you, anyway?"

Chuckling, he put my king in check yet again and flexed his muscles a bit under the pretext of stretching. "Six foot eight on a good day. You never answered my question about what you do with all your time."

I took out his offending rook with my queen then looked at him, trying to figure out the best thing to say to him. What would a guy like Seth Hastings want to hear? He'd probably love to have all his suspicions confirmed, so I could tell him I went to the outlets and got manicures and sat around sipping lattes in cafes talking about hair and hot gossip. He raised an eyebrow at me, as if goading me into doing just that, so I switched tactics.

"I travel all over the world," I said, folding my arms as he made his move. "I host great parties. I get really good at chess. Check," I added as I moved my queen into position and sent him a playful glare.

But Seth just grinned and moved his earring queen to attack mine. "Check mate," he replied.

"Let's play again," I said immediately.

CHAPTER EIGHT

By game three, I was really starting to get frustrated. I couldn't re-member the last time someone had beaten me at chess—though it had admittedly been a while since I played—and yet Seth kept cor-nering me before I could put any of my best strategies to use. And he didn't even seem to be concentrating as he kept up conversation, fo-cusing more on what we were saying than on the game.

"Will and I met when I was nine," he said as he chased my pieces around the board. "Dad wasn't all that fond of him, but he practically spent the whole summer at my house, since there was a lot more space to play Cops and Robbers than at his place."

I tried to make a play to get his earring queen, but he didn't fall for the bait and took out *my* queen instead. "Let me guess," I said, irritation in my voice. "You were always the robber."

Seth laughed. "How did you know?" he asked with sarcasm. "Will's wanted to be a cop since the day he was born, and the one time I sug-gested we switch places, he practically burst into tears and ran away. It still blows my mind that he can keep Geller believing he's one of them because there's nothing criminal about the guy."

I wasn't all that convinced Geller really did believe it, but I kept that suspicion to myself. It was better to think Will had at least some power to come to my rescue. So instead of imagining how Geller would take him out once Will was no longer useful, I tried to picture Seth as a little kid. It was pretty difficult, given his sheer size as he hunched at the table and surveyed the board.

I moved a pawn and said, "I wish I had had more friends growing up." Then I immediately regretted that when Seth looked up and gave me a piercing stare. *Let's not look into that too deeply*, I told him silently. "I switched schools a lot," I explained. "Hard to keep friends that way."

"Why?" he asked. "I mean, why did you change schools? Your dad has always lived in Maryland, hasn't he?"

How well did Seth know my dad? He obviously knew enough to know about me, but had he ever actually met dear old Dad? "We've been in Maryland for the last six years," I said. "Before that it was Virginia, but he grew up here in California. How do you—"

"Milton Davenport has done a lot of work with the Special Forces," Seth said. "Check."

I was too surprised by his comment to get annoyed that I was losing again. I knew Dad did something military related, but I didn't know how deep into it he got. "What does my dad do?" I asked without thinking.

Seth furrowed his brow. "You don't know?"

"He never tells me anything. He barely talks to me at all." And though I didn't know why Seth would want to hear this, I said it anyway: "He probably doesn't even know I was kidnapped, so why would he bother telling me what he does with his life?" I moved my king, but I was angry enough at my dad that I knocked it over. Groaning, I just left it lying sideways on the board and folded my arms. "You were going to win anyway," I mumbled.

Pretty motionless, Seth watched me for a moment then said, "Why don't you think your dad knows you're gone?" He was so quiet that I almost couldn't hear him.

I shrugged. "Because he only cares about himself and told me he wasn't going to answer his phone for anything. If I got myself into trouble, I would have to get myself out of it."

"Did you come to Tahoe by yourself?" He was looking at me as if I were a toddler and he was amazed I had managed to get on a plane without my daddy holding my hand.

A familiar resentment bubbled up inside me, and I sat there wondering how long Seth had been seeing me as a child. Was it when I told him I was eighteen? Or was it right from the beginning? "A driver took me to the airport and helped me get on the plane," I said bitterly.

"Then my cousin's husband was there to pick me up at the gate when I landed so I didn't get lost."

Clenching his jaw, Seth leaned back in his chair and scrutinized me the same way all adults did when they realized my actual age. Trying to understand how I had gotten this far without someone to help me with every step. "And now you're waiting for Will to come rescue you," he muttered.

"I don't need rescuing."

"So you hanging out in this cabin is your idea of a vacation?"

I jumped to my feet so I could be taller than him. "No," I snarled, "I'm stuck here because I'm not stupid enough to go out there in the middle of a blizzard. And no, my idea of a vacation is not being babysat by my lame cousins who apparently have nothing better to do than stop me from living my own life out in the world."

Though his expression didn't change, Seth cocked his head a little. "I don't think you're ready for the real world, Princess."

"Don't *call* me that!"

"Then don't act like that," he replied calmly. "You may have the rich world figured out, and you may know exactly which buttons to push to get your way, but that's not going to do you any good when you finally get out there in the world. You can't be a princess forever."

"What would you know?" I said sharply, though I could already tell my usual anger wasn't having any effect on the soldier who had seen too much real darkness to be moved by mine. But I couldn't seem to get myself back in control and find a better way to convince him I was worth more than he evidently thought. "You're just a dumb soldier."

Resting his cheek in his hand, he watched me as I clenched my fists, as if waiting for me to inevitably explode or break into tears or something else ridiculous. "For the record," he said quietly, "I don't believe your act."

"I don't have an act," I snapped.

"Yeah, you do. You need the world to think you're the best because you're so afraid to show them who you really are."

Something twisted painfully in my chest, and I stared at him, trying to decide why his words didn't feel as mean as his deep voice made them sound.

"This whole princess thing you've got going is probably the only way you know how to be, right?" he continued. "And your whole world is fooled by it, so they bow down at your feet and make you feel important."

I didn't like where he was going with this, but I couldn't find my voice to tell him so.

Seth kept his turquoise eyes locked on mine. "Let me tell you something I've learned over the years," he said. "The world doesn't care about you. Probably never will. No matter how intelligent, resourceful, beautiful you might be, everyone is just going to care about themselves, so you have to stop thinking you need to throw yourself in their path and expect not to get trampled. Your life is not just some game with you as the prize, Cat." He slowly got to his feet, which made his next words so much more powerful as he loomed over me: "You're worth so much more than they'll ever tell you. Stop pretending to be less than the incredible woman you are. You deserve more than what you've let yourself have."

And then he collapsed.

"Seth!" I shrieked and dropped to his side, but I had started crying at some point so I could barely see as I helped keep him upright on his knees.

"I'm okay," he whispered, but he was so pale that I worried he was going to pass out completely. He leaned heavily against me and kept his eyes shut tight. "I…" He took a long breath that looked incredibly painful based on the grimace that came with it. "I should probably lie down."

It wasn't easy, considering his sheer size, but together we managed to get him to the couch, though in my effort to help him fall into it slowly, I ended up wedged beneath his arm next to him. I tried to wiggle myself free, but he tightened his hold around me.

"Not yet," he begged, his eyes still closed. "I need the distraction."

If being snuggled up against his side wasn't ridiculously comfortable—and warm—I might have protested, but I just adjusted myself so I could rest my head against his broad chest and settled in. For a guy who was stuck in a tiny little cabin in the middle of the Sierras, he smelled amazing, and there was something in the way he held me that made me want to stay hidden in his embrace forever. I'd never felt so safe in my life.

"I see how it is," I said softly. "You just said those nice things about me so you could butter me up and use me as a distraction."

"Yes," he said through gritted teeth. "But I wouldn't have said them if they weren't true."

I had no idea how to respond to that, so I lifted the bottom of his shirt so I could check on his wound, since I was in a pretty good position to see it. It had bled a bit, but it seemed to be holding. "How does it feel?" I asked him.

He took a long, slow breath. "Feels like I got stabbed," he grunted. "So, you know, not too bad."

Good grief, he really was all muscle. I'd known models and fitness junkies, and none of them quite compared to Seth. It wasn't like he looked like those bodybuilders in the contests on TV, all misshapen and almost frightening to look at. No, Seth was simply *strong*. Strong, solid, warm, and immensely comfortable.

As I let my fingers rove over the healing cuts and bruises on his skin, I found a raised bump near his ribcage, an old scar about an inch long.

"Machine gun," Seth said, answering my unasked question.

"And this one?" I asked, finding another on the other side.

"Shrapnel."

He had a burn lower down, closer to his hip.

"An IED that took out half my squad," he said.

I sat up enough to touch the scar on his face near his right ear, one that looked a little newer than the rest, and then I met his unreadable gaze.

Without blinking, Seth leaned a little deeper into my touch and muttered, "Assault rifle," before closing his eyes again. A fraction of an inch closer, and that one would have killed him.

When he said he'd been injured a lot, he really wasn't kidding. I wasn't sure I had the heart to ask about the more recent injuries that littered his body. If the tabloid article was true and he'd been in the military since graduating Yale, he'd been fighting for four years, which meant he'd seen a whole lot of death and destruction in a very short amount of time. No wonder he had nightmares.

He fell asleep only a couple minutes later. I didn't blame him, and I carefully stretched him out along the couch, though he was too big to fit properly; his feet hung over the edge because he was just too dang tall. *And heavy*, I silently complained as I tried to shift him so his head rested on the soft armrest, but I couldn't really move him without jostling him enough to wake him. He looked awful, pale and gaunt, with the dark circles under his eyes just growing as the days went on, and he badly needed to sleep if he was ever going to heal. He may have been annoying and confusing and just a little bit terrifying, but I certainly didn't want the guy to die.

While he slept, I grabbed more wood from the blustery porch and made a neat little stack that would hopefully last us a while. That done, I went into the kitchen, considering making some soup again now that I knew what not to do, but instead I went back to washing dishes, though I kept my distance from any knives. There weren't many dishes to do, though, and I wasn't sure what else I could do to pass the time.

I had never liked being alone, and I was starting to wonder if Seth was the same way. If I had lived his life, I would have had a hard time keeping those nightmares away on my own. How had he gotten this far? Had he tried therapy or anything, or did he think he just had to live with his trauma?

I wandered back around the counter to the couch to look at him, but just as I reached him, he screamed.

I jumped, instinct sending me straight back into the bedroom. But as my heart pounded wildly in my chest, I forced myself to stop halfway, holding myself there at the edge of the hallway and listening to Seth beg for the lives of the innocent family. It was worse this time as he thrashed on the couch, though his arms seemed bound to his sides. His raw screams filled the small space of the cabin and penetrated deep into my chest until I could hardly breathe as I stood there. He was going to hurt himself. Tear his stitches, maybe worse, but I wasn't sure if there was anything I could do to help him. Even if he simply tried to protect me from the unseen horror, there was a high chance I would end up getting hurt.

"Seth," I whispered, my voice trembling and weak. "Seth, wake up." I made myself inch just a little closer, my uncut hand in a tight fist. I'd barely noticed the pain in my palm for the last little while, but it seemed to throb worse than ever as the soldier screamed.

"Stop," Seth begged. Blood had nearly soaked through the gauze on his belly, and a sickly sheen of sweat shone on every bit of skin I could see. His dreams were literally killing him. "Please, I'll do anything."

"Seth."

Then something shifted, and he grew still, though his breathing had only gotten faster, more desperate. His whole body seemed to tense as he lay there. Shaking. And I forced myself into the front room, pausing at the couch as I watched him. "Do it," he said, but he was hoarse from his scream. "Just kill me."

My knees gave out, and I sank to the floor with tears welling up in my eyes. This was so much worse. What had they done to him after they captured him? I didn't want to know, but he had a body full of injuries that told me anyway. "Seth, please wake up."

"I won't," he growled. "I won't tell you. You'll have to kill me. Please," he begged. And then he sat straight up and shouted, "Kill me!" with nothing but fear in the words.

I grabbed his hands, and he jerked his eyes open. "Seth," I whimpered.

He stared at me, his chest still heaving, and I wasn't sure if he had any idea where he was because he just stared at me with terrified eyes and muttered, "Make it stop. Please."

"Seth, you're okay."

"I can't…" Tears spilled from his eyes. "Please, I can't do any more."

I winced as his fingers tightened around mine, but I knew I couldn't stop talking to him. "Seth, it's me. It's Catherine. You're okay. No one is going to hurt you. I promise."

He blinked, and his focus seemed to sharpen as he sat there in the firelight. As if he were coming back to himself. "Catherine?" he whispered. Dropping my hands, he covered his head with his arms as his whole body shook. "I failed," he said. "I couldn't save them."

I brushed away tears, desperately searching for a way to help him. I'd never gone through something like he had. My life of luxury hadn't been easy, always having to be put together and confident and unshaken by the criticism that was always a step behind me, but I'd never experienced real trauma. Still, that didn't change the fact that I knew—oh did I know—how exhausting it could be to deal with everything on your own. "Seth," I whispered and gingerly put my hand over his on the back of his head. "It wasn't your fault."

He was still breathing so heavily, shaking so much that I could feel it in the floor beneath my knees.

"Seth, look at me."

He did, grabbing my hand as it fell from his head.

"Breathe," I said. I was pretty sure he tried, but his lungs hardly inflated as he sat there staring at me, so I lifted my injured hand and touched it to his chest. Then, moving as slowly as I could, I pressed his hand against my collarbone. "With me, okay?" I took a deep breath, relaxing a little when he did it with me. "Just keep breathing."

I didn't say anything until he'd taken several breaths in sync with mine, but he still looked half lost in his nightmare. I didn't know what made this one worse. With the other, he'd woken up so quickly, but as he sat there on the couch, me kneeling in front of him, he kept looking around the cabin as if expecting someone to hurt him still. I wasn't sure if he could get out of this one on his own.

"Seth?" I said, speaking as gently as I could. "Look at me."

He did, but he glanced away almost immediately.

"Hey." I placed a hand on either cheek and held his face toward me. "Just focus on me, okay? Can you do that? Focus." I wiped tears from his cheeks and tried to keep myself calm, though I was nearly breaking into sobs as I sat there. I didn't know what I was doing. Sure, I had my own experiences, but how was anything about my life supposed to help this broken soldier?

"Keep breathing with me," I told Seth, trying to find something in the room that could help, all the while trying to keep my eyes on his as much as possible. "Focus on my touch. The couch beneath you. The smell of the fire. The sound of my voice."

Seth was pretty fixated on me now, his breathing growing steady. But he still had so much fear in those turquoise eyes of his, as if any second he might slip back into the nightmare.

I leaned a little closer, hoping that would keep him present. "No one is going to hurt you, Seth," I said again. "You're safe here. You don't have to be afraid."

"But I am afraid," he admitted.

"I'm not," I replied. And I wasn't. This man wasn't going to hurt me.

Closing his eyes, Seth reached up and gently wrapped his fingers around my wrists, pulling my hands away from his face and holding them in his lap. "Maybe you should be," he said, his pain as clear in his words as it was in his face. "How…how did you do that?"

I relaxed a little, though I refused to move or look away, just in case. "All I did was talk to you," I said.

He shook his head. "You knew exactly what to do," he said, and he seemed to already know the answer to his question, even as he repeated it. "How?"

Even if we did get out of this cabin and he managed to get some real medical help, his nightmares weren't just going to stop. And it wasn't like my life could compare, but I talked anyway. If there was even a chance I could help him…

"When I was a kid," I said, "I used to get really bad panic attacks." I felt my chest constrict with the words, as if it was reminding me what that used to feel like. I didn't *want* to talk about it, but I knew I needed to. "It felt like the world was closing in around me. I couldn't breathe, and I thought I would fall apart, and the only thing that could calm me down was my mom. She'd hold me in her arms and breathe with me and help me ground myself in the world around me. After she died, I would just run from them because I couldn't let people know about them. They couldn't know I wasn't perfect."

He pulled his eyebrows together, his eyes taking me in. "Nobody's perfect," he said.

"Catherine Davenport is," I replied. "You can ask anyone. So if I could, I'd hide in the bathroom or outside or wherever I could be alone, and I had to pretend that my mom was there with me, talking me down and telling me that the world couldn't get to me. That I was better than that."

He frowned. "Catherine, that's not—"

"My dad barely acknowledged my existence from the moment I was born," I said. That part hadn't changed. But saying it out loud like this felt like I was tearing a hole in myself because I'd never been brave enough to admit it. This didn't have anything to do with helping him with his nightmares, but I couldn't seem to stop talking. "And after my mom was gone, the only way I felt like I was real was when people were admiring me. Because that meant I wouldn't be forgotten. I still existed, but only if people could see me. Only if I made absolutely sure everyone around me knew I was there."

Without shifting his soul-searching gaze, Seth lifted a hand and tucked some hair behind my ear. His fingers were cold. "I see you, Cat," he said, and for a moment it felt like nothing in the world existed but the two of us. "Thanks. For bringing me back. Without you…"

"You can breathe with me anytime," I whispered. Heat blossomed on my skin beneath his touch, and I slowly rose to my feet, intending to sit next to him on the couch again and slide back into his safe hold. But, as if on its own, my mind jumped to the magazine sitting on the end table where I'd left it after leaving the bathroom. That felt like days ago, but the picture of Seth and his very serious girlfriend was vivid in my thoughts.

Seth didn't need to be sitting in this cabin breathing with me; he needed to get back to the woman who loved him.

"You need to eat something," I said without preamble.

He blinked. "Catherine?"

"You're never going to heal if you don't have—"

He grabbed my hand as I turned toward the kitchen. "What's wrong?"

Flashing him a smile, I said, "Nothing's wrong," and pulled myself free.

But he was on his feet, blocking my way. "Yeah," he growled, "I don't believe that," and he nodded to my smile. "What…" He paused, his eyes sliding to the end table where I'd left the magazine in my search for him. "Oh my God, please tell me Will didn't keep that."

His reaction wasn't at all what I expected. His face red, he stared at the magazine until he forced himself to look back at me with wide eyes. Was he embarrassed? Seriously?

"You know that's all a bunch of bull, right?" he said as he pointed to the tabloid.

My own face burned with heat, mostly because of his tone. "It sounded pretty accurate," I mumbled, feeling almost sick as I tried to avoid Seth's gaze.

"When that thing came out," he said, "Will thought it was the funniest thing he'd ever read and bought a dozen copies. I thought I'd found them all the last time I was here and properly burned them, but apparently not."

He didn't have to rub my face in the fact that I believed it. "But you *were* born in California," I argued. I knew that much at least. "You moved to D.C. with your dad. You joined the Army." Let him argue *those*.

Seth actually laughed, drawing my gaze up to him in surprise. "I'm also apparently dating my sister," he said, lifting his eyebrows.

I stared at him. "What?"

"Lissa Montgomery." He nodded to the magazine. "That's my dear little sister."

"You said you didn't have any siblings," I argued.

Seth smiled wide and gently stroked my hair. "I said I was the only Hastings. I don't have siblings, technically. Not full ones, anyway, and none that Dad has ever actually acknowledged. I'm the only one he's ever claimed, though I'm pretty sure there are half a dozen of us running around various parts of the country."

I was so confused. "But your mom—"

"Works at a diner in Santa Rosa, and Thalia absolutely hates her. Hates me, in fact, though in public she plays the part of loving mother very well."

I felt so stupid standing there beneath his goofy grin, and yet I couldn't stop blushing as I gazed at him. He looked so different when he was happy, like he wasn't weighed down by his world as much as he normally was. The man standing in front of me looked a lot more like the one in the magazine and less like a tortured soul trying to hide from his troubles. And I couldn't look away.

I had to say something. Something to change the topic before Seth's expression turned to pity and he called me naive or childish or any number of things I had heard before. He may have switched into saying nice things, but I was pretty positive there were more insults lurking beneath the compliments.

For someone who didn't know me at all, he really did seem to know exactly who I was.

"You really should eat something," I muttered, lamely gesturing toward the kitchen.

Seth's smile faltered, but he managed to mostly keep it intact. Nodding a little, he turned toward the kitchen and muttered, "A good meal must begin with hunger."

Strange. "So you *are* hungry," I replied, following him around the counter as he pulled out a can of sauce and the rest of the package of conchiglie noodles from the cupboard.

Why was he suddenly grinning again? There was a hint of something mischievous in his eyes, which made me nervous. He seemed to be standing okay, not as much in pain or faint like before, but maybe he was going to have me attempt to cook again. I hadn't totally ruined the bacon, had I?

"To tell his illnesses often relieves," he replied.

Well that didn't make any sense. "Are you feeling okay?" I asked. "Are you getting sick?"

"You are a surprising one, Catherine."

I was way too tired to figure out why he sounded so weird. "Why am I surprising?" I was getting emotional whiplash from this guy.

Shaking his head, he grabbed a large pot and started filling it with water. "Did you actually hear what I said?" he asked and turned his gaze back to me with an eyebrow raised.

"Of course I did."

His expression didn't change. "Listen carefully," he said. "I'll repeat myself: A good meal must begin with hunger." Only he didn't say it in English. *Un bon repas doit commencer par la faim*, is what he actually said, and I thought back for a second, realizing with alarm he'd been speaking French the last few minutes and I hadn't even noticed.

"Wow," I breathed, "I *am* tired." *À raconter ses maux, souvent on les soulage*, he'd said. I'd heard the phrase before but had translated it literally in my exhaustion. "Do you want help with the cooking?" I asked and smiled a little as I repeated his little proverb in English: "A problem shared is a problem cut in half."

He shook his head, flipping on the stove and folding his arms as he waited for the water to boil. "Where did you learn to speak French so well?"

I shrugged. "Everyone learns French at my school."

"That level of comprehension, you're practically fluent."

I didn't know why he was watching me with such awe, but as I lifted myself up to sit on the counter, I really didn't want him to stop. That expression was one I was used to, and it made all of this feel more normal. "My nanny until I was twelve was from France," I said. "And I've been to Paris a dozen times."

"You know where Vientiane is," he said next, his eyebrows rising higher.

"Geography," I explained. Everyone had to take that in school, even at my fancy boarding school that focused more on appearances than it did academics.

"And I'm pretty sure you know Morse Code."

That one made me smile with pride. "When I was five, I had a neighbor Dad wouldn't let me play with. She and I both learned Morse Code so we could talk with flashlights through our windows at night."

Seth cursed under his breath, his eyes growing wide. "You learned Morse Code at five?" he asked. "Half my soldiers still don't know it. You speak two languages fluently and I would guess you probably know more than that." Spanish and German too, but who was counting? "You know more about Laos than I did until I got there. Why the hell aren't you doing my job?"

"Be a soldier?" I snorted. "No way."

"Do something good," he countered. "Save lives."

"I'm too busy trying to save my own life," I replied with a roll of my eyes. "Why would I bother with anyone else's?"

His expression shifted, hardening and becoming more like the soldier he usually was. While I didn't like seeing him without his smile, which seriously brought life back into his handsome face, I had no idea what I'd done to sober him so quickly, so I didn't know how to fix it. We'd been having a great conversation…

"What?" I asked.

Frowning, he dumped the noodles into the water before he turned back to me. "Don't yell at me this time, okay? Why do you insist on being the princess when you're clearly not?"

My heart sank. I was right about him. No matter what he might have said earlier, I was just a little girl to him. I spent all of my young life trying to live up to my dad's standards and never came up to par. I'd done everything I could to be a shining example of wealth and class, and still there was always someone better and prettier and more famous whose shadow was impossible to get away from. Was it so much to ask that someone just acknowledge me for who I was? "I'm trying my best," I muttered, feeling hollow and dizzy enough to need to rub my temples to ease the spinning.

"That's the problem," Seth replied, and to my surprise he stepped closer, adding his hands to mine. "Catherine…"

My heart seemed lodged in my throat. Even with my high perch on the counter, he still stood taller than me and had to lean down a little to look into my eyes. His own nearly glowed as he let his thumbs brush my hairline and kept his gaze firmly on me, and I had to try very hard to keep my lungs inflating before I passed out in his arms.

Seth couldn't seem to find his words as he stood there, his hip resting against my knee. He tried twice to say something and had to swallow and take a deep breath before he managed a soft, "Cat, you don't have to put all your energy into proving yourself to the world. You're better than that."

My heart, still in my throat, couldn't seem to decide if it wanted to race or stop altogether. No one had ever cared enough to talk to me like that. Hell, no one had ever *looked* at me like that, like he was seeing beneath the careful exterior I always tried so hard to keep flawless. To the world I had always been the perfect Catherine Davenport, a flirt and a beauty and heiress to a fortune. Nothing more. Here, sitting in a tiny kitchen in the middle of nowhere, I was *Cat*. And I desperately wanted to know who that was.

Holding my breath, I rested my hands against Seth's chest and felt his heart beating to match mine. He leaned in closer, and I followed his example until we were almost lip to lip. I had kissed so many men that I had lost count, but there in an old cabin, tasting his breath as I waited for him to close that final bit of distance, I realized I had never cared if a man kissed me. There would always be another to take his place. But I *needed* Seth to kiss me. There wasn't anyone out there who could even compare, and he was the first person who actually saw me instead of my mask.

Seth finally brushed his lips against mine, sending a shiver through me with just that brief touch. My hands found his neck and pulled him closer, and his kiss immediately deepened, becoming more intense by the second. His hands slid to my waist, and I pushed my fingers into his thick hair, and I couldn't have imagined anything better as I lost myself in his kiss. And I needed more.

"Cat," Seth whispered when my hands moved to the bottom hem of his shirt. "Catherine, wait." He took my fingers, keeping his forehead pressed to mine though he pulled away slightly. Maybe he wasn't up for it. With his injury…

"I'll be gentle," I assured him and slid more into his arms.

Seth took me by the shoulders and stepped back, his eyes full of concern. I didn't like that. "Catherine," he said, and his face only saddened more. "Who told you you had to grow up so fast?"

My heart sank into my stomach like a rock, cold and heavy and completely empty. For a minute there, I had thought he actually saw me as an equal. But no. *A child.* That was all I was to him, and I was stupid enough to think he could look past that like everyone else seemed to. Tears stung my eyes as I sat there wondering why the one person I wanted to see *me* could only see the girl I hadn't been in years.

Seth groaned and reached out to stroke my hair.

I grabbed his wrist.

"Cat, please. I didn't mean…"

"I know exactly what you meant," I said. Breath catching, I slid from the counter and went straight to my hiding place in the bedroom without bothering to close the door behind me. I'd thought Seth wouldn't hurt me, but he'd just dealt me a fatal blow. He didn't want me. I was just a child to him, and he didn't want me.

No one did.

"Catherine."

I curled up my knees to my chest as I sat on the bed and stared at the wall. Seth stood in the doorway, but I refused to look at him. "Why don't you want to be with me?" I whispered as tears slid down my cheeks. "I know I'm only eighteen, but I... I'm not just..." Not just a child. Maybe I didn't have experience in this regard, but I had grown up enough to know what I wanted. Why couldn't he see that? "Why don't you want me?"

I expected him to come into the room, sit on the edge of the bed and put a hand on my shoulder. But he didn't leave the doorway. He just stood there in the hall, because apparently he had no desire to get close to me again. "Catherine," he said, "it's not a matter of wanting you. I shouldn't have..." He let out a breath. "I shouldn't have kissed you, and I'm sorry."

I'm sorry. It was all anyone ever said to me. *I'm sorry, but you're too young. I'm sorry, but there's no way I'm making Milton Davenport my enemy. I'm sorry, but no one likes you—they're just pretending because you're rich.* I was growing sick of it because no one ever meant it. "Just stay away from me," I said, and I saw him flinch out of the corner of my eye. I'd said that to him enough over the last few days for him to understand perfectly.

"Cat..."

"Just go."

And he did. Without another word, he disappeared, leaving me completely alone. Like I always was.

Refusing to let myself cry, I sat there on the bed and stared at the wall as I relived the last hour. What had I done wrong? We had talked easily. Shared secrets. Smiled together. He said he was impressed by the things I knew, told me I was intelligent and surprising. He even told me I was beautiful. And while he may have been older than me, I knew my kissing skills weren't those of a child, so why didn't he want me? Why could he only see my age and not *me*?

His figure blocked out the hallway light when he returned, but I still refused to look at him. "You should eat," he said, bending down and setting a bowl of pasta on the floor just inside the room. "You need your strength as much as I do."

Just leave, I silently begged, too emotionally drained for words. *I don't need you to look after me. I don't need anyone.*

"Catherine, I'm sorry. I didn't mean to hurt you, and it's not that I don't want you. You have to believe me."

I closed my eyes, hoping that was enough to make him go back to his couch.

"Look, I know what it's like to be forced to grow up. To not have a normal childhood. People like us… We're told we have to be better than everyone else, and we lose our chance to just be kids and enjoy life. I don't want that for you. You still have a chance to be young. A chance to have a normal, simple life. Simple, Catherine. You deserve that."

I lost my chance for a simple life when my mom died, leaving me in the hands of a man who only cared that I didn't embarrass him. Even if I wanted to be a kid, it was too late for that. Too late for me. I couldn't change who I was. I couldn't change my world.

Seth sighed. "You've been through a lot these last few days. You've been hurt, and frightened, and ripped from your life. I didn't want… I don't want to take advantage of that. You should… You should get some sleep."

I looked up just as he left, leaving me feeling more alone than I'd ever been in my life.

CHAPTER NINE

I woke to sunlight streaming in through the window, right into my face, which didn't help the ache that pounded in my head from crying all night. While I thankfully hadn't had any horrible dreams after curling up beneath the blankets, the night had left me feeling even more tired than before. I just wanted to go home. I wanted this whole thing to be over so I could get back to my normal life and pretend none of it had happened. I wanted…

I blinked, looking at the bright window and trying to understand why it felt so strange to have sunlight—The storm! It stopped!

I jumped up, leaping over the pasta bowl I hadn't touched and sliding into the front room, which had more windows than the bedroom. The whole room was bathed in brightness and warmth that for once had nothing to do with the glowing embers in the fireplace. The snow had stopped, and that meant I could leave!

"Seth," I gasped, grabbing his shoulder where he slept on the couch and only realizing what a terrible idea that was when he jerked awake.

Luckily, he didn't jump up and grab me, just stared at me in alarm. "What's wrong?" he asked, fighting to sit up. "What happened?"

I couldn't help but smile. "The storm stopped. We can leave!"

Rubbing exhaustion from his face—he looked awful in the natural light—he turned to squint at one of the windows. "It stopped," he said.

"That's what I said, genius." Where had I seen those boots? And I had Will's thin coat still, which would be enough until I could get down the mountain and back into town. Snatching up the boots, I didn't even care that I didn't have enough socks to make them fit. I could finally leave this miserable place.

Seth stared at me as I sat on the floor and started lacing up the boots. "What are you doing?" he asked, still very much asleep, apparently.

"I'm getting out of here." *Obviously.*

"Catherine, you can't just wander out into a place you've never been before. Especially in boots that don't fit and half a coat."

"I'll be fine. I'll follow the road, and—"

"You should wait until Will comes," he argued.

I froze, last night returning to me with more clarity than I would have liked. "Why?" I snapped. "Because I'm just a little girl and can't do anything on my own?"

Groaning, Seth rubbed his face again and looked even more dead than usual, his skin almost gray beneath the pale. "That's not what I said."

"That's what you were thinking." The boots were big, yes, but as I stood and took a couple steps, I decided it wouldn't be completely awful. They might even make it easier to walk through the fresh snow, being as big as they were. Kind of a snowshoe effect.

"Catherine, don't…"

He paused as I gave him my best glare, the one I used to tell people they had no hope of changing my mind once I set myself on the path I wanted. It was a look that had gotten me gifts and drinks and free plane tickets and to backstages of concerts. It had yet to fail me.

Sighing, Seth shook his head and glanced out the window again. "Will you at least wait for me to come with you? I have an idea where the road goes so you don't end up waltzing off a cliff."

A babysitter. Exactly what I wanted. "Sure," I lied, folding my arms.

He raised an eyebrow, probably expecting more resistance than that, but I kept my expression perfectly neutral. *Let him try to decipher that!*

"Are we going to just stand here or are we going to get out of here?" I asked.

"Give me a few minutes," Seth replied and moved slowly to the bathroom. He was still really weak, which was a shame for him but great for me. His lack of energy would give me plenty of time to get a head start, and hopefully I would never have to see the man again.

The moment the bathroom door closed, I slipped out the front door and into the blinding sunlight, letting myself take one deep breath before I shoved off into the drifted snow. I could see a clear break in the trees that was probably the road. As long as I kept myself in the open area, I shouldn't have a problem finding my way down.

"See?" I said to myself as I pushed forward. "I don't need anyone's help. I'm fine on my own." Except the boots were causing a slight problem as snow kept slipping inside every time I sunk a few feet into the fresh powder. Still, it was better than no shoes at all. As long as I kept walking, I didn't have to worry *too* much about my feet going numb, and the snow was quickly packing down inside around my feet, serving as a useful buffer to keep them on tight.

Thank goodness there was no wind. The coat was really more of a jacket, and every slight breeze cut right through the fabric and added a chill to my skin. "Just keep walking," I told myself. The effort of shoving through a few feet of snow would soon heat me up just fine, since I was already starting to sweat from the exertion. I idly wondered if Will had any actual snowshoes at his cabin, but it was too late to go back. I was never going to set foot in that cabin again. *Ever.* I was done with all of it, and as soon as I got back to civilization, I was going to leave California behind and never come back there either. Not even the many vineyards could draw me back, no matter how great their wines were said to be.

Seth was from wine country.

"I'm never drinking wine again," I muttered, since talking seemed to keep my lips from freezing. Despite the sun, it was still alarmingly cold.

And bright. The fresh snow reflected the sunlight right into my face, and I had to squint just to see where I needed to go. The road turned to the right up ahead. Or maybe it went left… A meadow or some other clearing sat right in front of me, and there weren't enough trees to fully distinguish which way the road went.

"Right," I decided after a moment of studying the landscape. "It makes the most sense for it to go right."

Somehow it kept getting colder. The longer I walked, the more I sweat, and each little brush of wind seemed to turn every inch of me to ice. "You're fine," I assured myself. "This is California, not Alaska. If people can survive Alaskan winters, you can handle a little cold for an hour or two. You're…"

I paused, squinting at the landscape full of trees in front of me. Maybe I'd taken a wrong turn. I probably should have grabbed the map, though I couldn't fully remember where I'd left it. I could almost picture it if I closed my eyes, but the trail I'd followed from the warehouse hadn't been much of a road, and it came up from the other direction. Had I looked at the rest of it long enough to remember which way the road took?

I chose to backtrack, just in case. It was still early morning, so I had all day to find my way down the mountain if I needed it. I knew being out in the elements at night wasn't a good idea, so as long as I focused on—

My foot suddenly slipped in the snow and pulled me down the slope a couple of feet, though I managed to keep myself mostly in place by tensing and holding completely still. When had it gotten so steep? I hadn't been paying attention, too focused on what was ahead. "Stupid Catherine," I whispered, looking around for something to grab onto. The closest tree was too far away, but there was a bush half covered in snow not too far. If I could just stretch up a little and reach it…

I slipped another few feet down the hill and only managed to stay in place by plunging my hands into the snow. Fear crept into my chest as my higher leg started to shake from holding me up, while my other boot slipped right off my foot, leaving my damp sock exposed. I wasn't exactly on the edge of a cliff, but the slope was steep enough and icy enough that I could end up dragging across one of the jagged rocks below or slamming into a tree, and I couldn't picture either of those situations turning out very well for me.

"Think, Catherine," I said, but I was unprepared for this. I had no supplies or gloves or even a proper coat, and if I ended up at the bottom of the hill, I wasn't entirely sure if I would make it back up again. What had I done? I could imagine the headline when—if—someone eventually found me, most likely after the snow thawed in the spring: *Teenage Imbecile Found Dead Near Lake Tahoe Because She Didn't Have Sense to Stay Put.*

"Sorry I'll be the one putting the name to shame instead of my cousins," I told Dad, glancing down at the dangers below me. He probably wouldn't even realize I was dead until they found me. I half wondered if he would even care.

"Seth," I said next, because he really was my only hope. My arms started to shake like my leg, and my hands burned from the cold as I kept them deep in the snow to hold me in place. Seth would come find me.

But what if he had given up on me? I wouldn't blame him if he stepped out of that bathroom to find me missing and just threw his hands up, choosing to be rid of me. Why was I so freaking determined to do everything on my own? He had proven I didn't have to, and I wasn't capable anyway. Clearly. Anytime I'd tried to take care of myself, it had only led to disaster.

"Seth, I need you."

My right leg was cramping beneath me, my left stretched too far below me to be of any use. If I moved even a little, I knew I'd lose my grip and end up at the bottom of the slope, bruised or bloodied or worse. I'd lasted this long, against a homicidal art thief/terrorist and a soldier with sometimes violent PTSD and a goddamn blizzard, just to get myself killed by my own stupidity. It was a fitting end, I supposed, for someone who didn't even know who she was let alone how to take care of herself.

I couldn't hold myself up much longer. My hands were numb, and my leg was about ready to slip, and tears ran down my cheeks as I tried to tell myself everything was going to be okay. Even if I knew it wasn't. I'd always been a good liar, but I seemed to have lost that skill over the last few days.

"I'm sorry," I whispered. To Seth, to myself, to my family. I hadn't made life easy on anyone, and now they were going to have to deal with my frozen corpse, assuming they ever found me. I doubted they would mourn for me. Dad would be happy he didn't have to use his fortune to cover up my stupidity anymore. Lanna could get back to her blissfully happy life with her perfect husband instead of babysitting, and Matthew could try to find love instead of chasing down a stupid teenager; he deserved his own life. And Seth…

My leg gave out, pulling me down and tearing my hands from their holes in the snow. Gravity pulled me faster and faster through the ice and snow until a solid wave of pain brought me to a sudden halt and I had just enough air to say, "I'm sorry."

* * *

I'd never been in so much pain in my life. Every breath was agony, and I felt like even if I wanted to move, doing so would only make the pain worse. What surprised me was the warmth of it all, so different from the cold I'd expected. Had I been buried in snow? I wasn't sure how long I'd been unconscious, but if another storm came up and covered me, it might be warm beneath the snow.

Maybe I was already dead.

No, I wouldn't be in this much pain if I were dead. They said Heaven was supposed to be peaceful. A relief. Not… Who was I kidding? There was no way I was going to Heaven. I just had to hope I wasn't dead and that the pain was me clinging to life.

My whole body was broken, I was sure of it. Trees tended to do that to objects moving at high speeds. But I couldn't remember where I'd hit, the front or the back, and my inability to move was concerning. Not that it mattered, since no one was going to find me before I froze to death anyway.

Except it really was warm. A little too warm. My lungs burned every time I inhaled, the smell of smoke strongly mixed with something familiar that I couldn't quite place. Smoke? That didn't make sense. Was the whole mountain on fire? Seth! I needed to warn him. If he didn't know the fire was coming, he'd be trapped, and…

I opened my eyes as the panic that had filled me so quickly disappeared almost as suddenly. Yes, there was fire, but it was small. Contained in a box of metal and crackling cheerfully. I didn't understand.

Not until I realized I couldn't move because a large arm kept me securely in place, fingers wrapped protectively near my elbow. *Seth.* He'd found me.

When I'd sat with him yesterday, I had never felt safer. This, lying on the couch with his soft breaths brushing the top of my hair, was infinitely better. Even with the pain that still kept me from breathing, I knew nothing could happen to me. As long as I stayed in that embrace, everything would be okay.

Suddenly he stirred behind me, and though I hadn't moved even an inch, he seemed to sense a change in me. "Catherine?" he said in alarm and shifted his weight to check on me.

His arm pressed down on my ribcage, pulling a soft, "Ow," out of me, though I couldn't help but smile.

His relief was palpable, washing over me as he dropped his head against mine. "Thank God," he whispered. "You stopped breathing."

"It hurts too much," I replied.

Lifting his arm, he raised himself up just enough so I could see his face, though there was barely room on the couch for both of us and I worried I would fall off if he moved too much. He looked so worried, and I wanted to smooth the lines out of his forehead. But that would require moving, and I wasn't ready for that yet. "Where does it hurt?" he asked, sounding almost desperate.

"Everywhere."

He brushed some hair from my forehead before pressing his lips to my temple. "I was so afraid you weren't going to wake up," he said, his voice strained. And then he seemed to realize where he was, and his expression turned even more pitiful as he muttered, "I'm sorry," and started to get up.

"No," I begged, reaching out for his arm. Just that little movement sent a shock of pain through my torso, enough that I had to shut my eyes before the dizziness made me black out again. "Don't…don't leave. Please." There was no way I could face the pain alone.

After a moment's hesitation, Seth carefully settled back against me, though he didn't drape his arm over me like before. Instead, he just brushed his fingers along my arm, which was deliciously distracting. "You were shivering," he said quietly, as if I needed an explanation for why he was there next to me. "I was worried you…"

Tears of pain leaked from the corners of my eyes, and I focused on the feel of his gentle touch. "What happened?" I asked.

"An idiot girl thought she could slide down the mountain instead of taking the road," he replied, though he accompanied it with a kiss to the top of my head. "You hit a tree."

"I know," I said. "I was there."

Seth's laugh was gentle, and it eased my pain just a little bit. Until his voice broke as he said, "You were barely breathing, and I thought… I thought I'd lost you, Cat."

I pushed myself deeper into his embrace, and he once again wrapped me in his hold as we lay there. *I could spend the rest of my life in his arms*, I thought and closed my eyes. "I'm sorry," I whispered. "I'm so sorry."

"You might have some broken ribs," he said. "Probably a concussion. And your foot…"

What was wrong with my foot? Ignoring the pain in my neck and chest, I lifted my head enough to see my right foot sticking out at the strangest angle, like it was hardly attached to my leg. Either I had so much pain everywhere that I hadn't even noticed, or I'd injured it enough that it was completely numb. "Well that's a problem," I muttered lightly.

Seth's laugh, soft though it was, was the most beautiful sound I'd ever heard. "You, darling, are the most remarkable girl I've ever met." Being absolutely careful not to jar me too much, he shifted me enough that I could look up into his face again. His mouth was dangerously close to mine, and the look in his eyes made my heart pound as he slowly moved closer.

"What happened to me being too young for you?" I asked, regretting the words immediately. *Stupid Catherine!*

But Seth didn't move. He even smiled a little. "I never said that," he replied.

"You regretted it the last time." *Stop talking, idiot.*

Seth shook his head, and his lips very nearly touched mine. "I never said that either." He was waiting. Waiting for me to let him know that he could, that I wanted him to.

Oh, did I want him to. I reached up, touching the scar on his face and leaving my fingers against his cheek. He closed his eyes, holding his breath, and I couldn't imagine a more perfect moment than that.

The blood was a bit of a complication, though.

"Seth," I said in alarm.

He barely moved, his eyes still shut. "Hmm?"

I could feel it soaking into my hip, startlingly wet. And Seth was paler than usual as his whole body shook behind me. "Seth."

He fell back against the couch, his breaths short and fast. "Yeah, that's not good," he mumbled.

Though moving was agony, I rolled from the couch and knelt next to him, my breath catching as I realized just how much blood he'd lost. Why hadn't he said something? "You carried me back," I said in horror, lifting the bandage to discover he'd torn nearly all his stitches, and blood oozed from his wound like it was brand new. He'd barely been able to stand up for more than a few minutes before, and trekking out into the snow and climbing that hill with me in tow had probably been the worst possible thing he could have done.

"Seth, why didn't you tell me?"

He could barely manage to open his eyes to look at me. "Didn't matter," he said, hardly above a whisper.

Didn't matter? "Seth, you're dying." He was dying, and I didn't know how to fix it. "You need a hospital." *The phone.* Maybe with the storm gone, it would work now.

Dragging myself across the floor was agony. Every movement sent fire flashing across my ribs. Every inch made the pain in my foot slowly grow until it definitely existed. I could barely breathe, could barely see through the pain, but I pulled myself across the floor anyway because Seth needed me to. I practically clawed at the wood beneath me as I went, and when I finally reached the kitchen, I was sure I couldn't handle any more. But I still had to get to the phone, which hung on the wall higher than I could reach, and I wasn't sure I had the strength to pull myself up, not after my crawl across the room. But I heard a gasp of pain behind me, and I forced myself to keep moving because I knew he didn't have much time left. I grabbed the edge of the counter and heaved, groaning against the pain as I lifted myself up just high enough to hook my finger around the phone's cord and tug, tearing the phone from its holder. As it clattered to the floor beside me, I took an agonizing breath and reached for the receiver.

But another hand reached for it before I could get it, and I turned to Seth to ask him why he wasn't staying on that couch and keeping himself alive just a little longer.

Only it wasn't Seth who grinned at me as he replaced the phone on the wall.

Max Geller had found me at last.

CHAPTER TEN

"H uh," Geller said, as if he'd just stumbled across a mildly interesting piece of trivia. How had he found me? What happened to Will? "I was half expecting to find you dead in a corner," he said, looking me over. "Will said you'd be here, but he didn't seem convinced I would be happy when I got here."

Will said… He'd betrayed me? After all that time telling me he would keep me safe, he had told Geller exactly where to find me.

"That doesn't look very good, Miss Davenport," he continued, crouching right in front of me. He touched my broken foot, and I couldn't hold back a cry of pain. Pain and fear. I had nowhere to hide. No way to run. "Oh, don't worry," he said, "I won't make you walk on it. That would only slow us down, and you're worth more intact than in pieces anyway."

How could anyone sound so cold? I'd been frightened of him before, but now I couldn't even find my voice. He was entirely in control here, and I had no way to fight him.

"This one, on the other hand…" Straightening up, Geller stepped over to the couch and leaned over the back of it as if he were having a casual conversation with some friends. "It's nice to see you again, Sergeant."

Seth's eyes were wide as he stared up at Geller, though I didn't think he had the energy to say anything. But the fear in his face was worse than seeing his blood. Seth was absolutely terrified, which meant I'd been right. The two of them hadn't met in the US, and they'd recently crossed paths in Southeast Asia.

"Don't hurt him," I begged from my spot on the floor.

Geller looked at me with nothing but amusement in his eyes. "Hurt him?" he asked, as if I'd suggested something ridiculous. "No, I plan to kill him."

"Why?" I gasped. What had Seth done to him?

Geller laughed. "Because it didn't work the first time, obviously."

"Get out of here, Cat," Seth whispered, turning his eyes to me.

I didn't move, not that I really could have. There was no way I was leaving him behind.

"Please," he begged.

"This is adorable," Geller said, his eyes alight with amusement. "You really are America's golden hero, aren't you? Desperate to save anything that moves. That's why you're in this mess in the first place, you know. Too much in the spotlight not to get noticed. If you would just tell us where dear Daddy is hiding out, I could just end your suffering and let you die in peace."

So he did want Seth's dad. But it was a lot of trouble to go through for the Secretary of Homeland Security.

"You look confused," Geller said, turning his attention back to me and making me tremble with fear. But at least he wasn't standing over Seth anymore. If I could just keep his attention on me, maybe I could keep Seth safe. "And I really hate it when the bad guy in the movies wastes so much time telling all the secrets of his big plan, but I have nowhere to be, my men are outside, and I don't think either of you can do anything anyway. This sounds like fun."

I shrieked as Geller grabbed my arm, dragging me across the floor to the couch. I immediately took Seth's frighteningly cold hand and watched Geller pull up a chair near the fireplace, blocking my access to the door. As he sat, I saw a gun tucked in his belt and knew it was only a matter of time before he used it.

"Once upon a time," Geller said, and he laughed as if he'd just told a fantastic joke, "there was a little soldier who was just a bit too good at his job."

Seth tried to squeeze my hand, but he failed miserably in the attempt. He was fading, and fast.

"He kept poking his nose into other people's business and started to catch on to a project he shouldn't have." Geller paused to make sure I understood the story, and then he smirked. "This whole storytelling thing is a lot more fun than I expected. Who knew?"

I squeaked, not sure what I could say but wanting to stop him from telling whatever horrible story I knew was coming.

Geller just sneered down at me. "When these people realized who this soldier was, or who his daddy was, they stopped trying to kill him from a distance"—my stomach clenched—"and went for a different plan. If they caught the little soldier, they could get his daddy to do whatever they wanted, which was a valuable asset to have. Only the little soldier's dad turned out to be a bastard and just laughed when they sent a ransom video."

I glanced at Seth, but he'd closed his eyes. Or maybe he'd passed out already.

"So they decided to make the little soldier tell them how to catch his daddy because the son of a bitch vanished," Geller continued, his tone growing more and more patronizing. "But the little soldier was brave, and he kept his mouth shut for days even though they tried everything to get him to talk."

I was going to be sick. Holding Seth's hand as tight as I could, I tried to keep my fear from showing on my face. I had to be strong for Seth, and maybe I could figure out a way to get him out of this.

Geller chuckled and sat back in his chair, completely at ease though his eyes sparked with anger. "One day," he continued, "the little soldier managed to escape from his cage and hop on a private plane headed for California, where he disappeared until I walked through the door of a quaint little cabin and found him dying right before my eyes. And even better, I think you, Miss Davenport, are going to be more useful than I originally planned."

In a flash, Geller leapt forward and grabbed me, pulling me against his chest and pressing his gun to my temple.

"No!" Seth cried, but his attempts to get up only left him paler than before. "Don't hurt her," he moaned even as his pain threatened to overwhelm him. "Please, God, don't hurt her. I'll do anything. Tell…tell you anything."

"I should have known it would be that easy," Geller growled in my ear. "I'm sure you have all sorts of cowards wrapped around your finger, don't you, Princess?"

I could barely balance on my good foot, and a sharp pain in my chest made breathing almost impossible. But I kept my eyes locked on Seth, trying to find a way to tell him everything would be okay. He didn't have to save me. *Please don't try to save me.* I wasn't worth it.

I just wished he would have figured that out before he carried me back.

I felt strangely calm as I stood there. It could have been because of the lightheadedness from not being able to breathe, but I wasn't afraid. Not anymore, and I wasn't sure why. Maybe because there was nothing I could do to stop Seth from dying, and I likely wasn't going to last very long once Geller got his ransom, so there was no point in fighting anymore. We'd already lost.

Check mate.

But Seth set his jaw, and I could see his determination even before he started to sit up. "If you hurt her," he snarled, and the temperature in the room seemed to drop several degrees with his words, "I swear to God you'll beg for me to kill you."

Geller snorted. "You can't even stand up, Hastings," he said, but there was a new edge to his voice. An undercurrent of fear.

Seth seemed to be putting every bit of energy he had left into his movement, forcing himself up to his feet even though he looked barely conscious. And when he was standing tall, he lifted his hands and pointed a gun at Geller. Where had that come from? Had he had that the whole time? "I only have to shoot you once," he growled.

Geller shifted behind me, using me as a shield. "You won't risk her life," he said.

Seth didn't budge. "Are you willing to risk yours?" His eyes met mine, so fierce and fiery that I almost believed he was strong enough to actually do something. But I knew better, and I knew that his gaze was telling me two very specific things: *I'm sorry. Run.*

For once, I listened. I threw my elbow into Geller's chest and dove for the open door at the same time a gunshot echoed around me. My shoulder collided with the door as I fell and pulled it with me, shutting it behind me as I tumbled into the snow and the silence.

"Seth!" I gasped, but I could barely move. I could barely *breathe*. It felt like my lungs had stopped working entirely, and the pain was so intense I could hardly think. There was only one gunshot. But whose had it been?

Someone stepped into my line of sight and looked down at me, one of Geller's men, but the man behind him was focused on the cabin. If Seth wasn't already dead, he would be as soon as the other thieves went inside.

"Grab the girl!" Geller shouted as he burst through the door.

No. Seth! My vision was dimming, and the orange sunset looked like fire in the sky.

The man closest to me reached out his hand, but an explosion knocked him off his feet. Another gunshot? But it came from the wrong direction. I didn't understand.

"Catherine!" The familiar voice echoed in my head.

"No!" Geller cried, but a second explosion burst through my ears at the same time he fell into the snow.

Shapes darkened the orange glow around me, more people than I could count, but I wasn't sure I would last long enough to find out which side they were on.

"Catherine," that same voice said. "Please talk to me."

I couldn't. I needed air to talk.

"She can't breathe! Someone help!"

What was Matthew doing in the mountains?

"Help," I whispered. Seth needed help.

"You'll be okay," Matthew told me.

And maybe he was right. But Seth wasn't okay, and the world faded to black before I could tell my cousin to save him instead of me.

CHAPTER ELEVEN

I woke in a fog, my mind and body both numb, though an ache still echoed in my center. I'd been in a hospital before, but it was strange to wake up there with no recollection of anything that happened before. I knew only two things as I lay there: Matthew had found me, and Seth was dead.

The first fact was surprising. Especially after the way I acted, I hadn't expected him to try. But somehow my cousin found me outside a random cabin in the middle of the Sierras. The second fact didn't hurt as much as I expected it to. Maybe it was because Seth had been dying from the moment I met him, so it wasn't unexpected. Maybe it was because I'd only known him for three days, and it wasn't like I was in love with the man.

So why did I feel so completely empty?

Someone sat near my bed, his face in his hands and his mop of black hair a complete mess. Some scrapes and bruises lined his knuckles, and some poked out on his face between his fingers, but he was very much alive and in one piece.

I spoke his name with anger, though I could hardly get the word out: "Will."

His head snapped up, eyes wide. "Catherine," he gasped.

I didn't want him there. I didn't want to see his face, especially because it looked like he'd run headlong into a truck and bruised every inch of it. "You told him where to find me," I whispered. "You were supposed to protect me, and you led him right to me."

Will paled beneath the purple, barely breathing as he fought for something to reply. And I watched him, daring him to try to convince me otherwise. "It's not that simple," he said. That wasn't a denial.

Simple. Was anything in life actually simple? I used to think so, but now I wasn't so sure.

"Go away, Will," I said because I had no way to force him to leave.

The man had the nerve to stay there and pretend I'd said nothing. What was the point of having a private hospital room if I couldn't choose who stayed and who didn't? "Catherine, I didn't have a choice. He found out who I was, knew I'd helped you get away. He nearly killed me."

So he was nothing more than a coward. I should have seen that from the beginning when he refused to get me home. The man left me alone in a cabin with barely any food and no knowledge of how to survive through a blizzard. Seth wouldn't have... I swallowed as the pain I hadn't felt yet burst to life deep in my chest. Some sort of drug kept my physical pain at bay, but it could do nothing to help the hollow ache that might never go away.

"I don't want to talk about this," I told Will and closed my eyes, hoping it would get him to leave.

"Don't fall asleep yet," he replied. Why couldn't he just disappear? "Your cousin will want to know you're okay." He rose to his feet and slipped out the door without giving me a backward glance.

My cousin. Matthew had found me, brought me to safety. Would I ever be able to thank him?

But it was Lanna who stepped into the room, her eyes red with tears as she rushed to my side. "Catherine," she said and grabbed my hand. "I'm so glad you're okay. I was so worried you..." She couldn't finish her thought and simply started crying again.

I matched her, using what little strength I had to squeeze her fingers. "I'm so sorry," I said through my tears. She looked like she hadn't slept since I was taken, and those sunken eyes were my fault. But even as we cried together, I couldn't help but feel a strange warmth inside me. While I hadn't exactly given her any reason to miss me, she was worried about me. Worried enough to lose sleep over me. I doubted even my father had ever thought about me like that. Speaking of...

"My dad?" I asked.

Wiping her cheeks, Lanna shook her head. "We, uh, haven't been able to get ahold of him." Of course they hadn't. Dad wouldn't answer the phone for anything. Not even if his only child were in mortal danger. "Adam's been in touch with his hotel," she added and gave my hand a little squeeze. "I'm sure he'll call soon. But you can stay with us as long as you need...or want to."

If I had any courage to tell her, I'd stay with her forever. Lanna's family felt so much more comfortable than my own, like they actually wanted me there. Even when I was causing trouble or making things difficult. After the few days I'd just had, I had no desire to spend any time alone if I could help it.

My eyes traveled down to the blankets tucked around my body. Without the pain, I wasn't completely sure how injured I actually was. "What happened?" I asked, looking back at Lanna.

"Matthew saw Geller lead you from the party," Lanna said carefully, and she traced comforting little circles along the back of my hand as she spoke. "Before he could get to you, the power went out in the building. He couldn't get out of the chaos, and by the time he reached the parking lot, you were gone."

"So was the painting," I added. The one that was worth a literal fortune.

Lanna shrugged. "I don't care about the painting. None of us do. We were worried about you. The security cameras could only give us so much information, and we had no idea where to look. I've never been so scared in my life."

"Will helped me escape," I said. Though it didn't do me much good in the long run… I just ended up with a miserable few days and a battered and broken body. And an even more broken heart with a hole I didn't know how to fill. I wasn't even sure what was missing.

Seth was missing. And unless I figured out what that feeling was when he held me, that warmth and safety, I wouldn't be able to fix myself.

Nodding a little, Lanna took a slow, exhausted breath and fiddled with my blankets. "Matthew was using every resource he had to try to find you. Adam called in favors. And I felt completely useless because there was nothing I could do to bring you back home."

Home. That was the feeling I was missing.

"Catherine, what happened to you? At the cabin. Officer Dunn said you made it up there just fine, and then Matthew got up there and you were…"

Broken. In every possible way. And while I had no desire to relive nearly everything that happened in that cabin, I couldn't let Lanna keep worrying over me by not knowing. I would just leave out certain details. Gloss over some moments so I could keep them to myself. "Will helped me escape the warehouse where Geller took me, and I found his cabin so I could hide out until it was safe." *Or until he cracked and made all of it pointless by telling Geller where to find me.* "I talked to him on the radio at one point, but the storm made leaving impossible."

"And how did you…" She winced, glancing at my battered body beneath the blanket. "How did you break your ribs? Your ankle? When Geller found you, did he…?"

"I slipped in the snow," I admitted, hating myself for it. If I hadn't been a complete idiot, Seth wouldn't have had to come after me, and he wouldn't have made his injury worse. He might have been able to fight Geller if not for me. "Hit a tree," I said, and my voice cracked. "Broken ribs?"

Nodding, she repeated a list of injuries as if she'd told herself many times she was to blame for them. Could she be any more perfect? "You have six broken ribs," she said. "One of them punctured your lung and made it collapse. You have two fractures in your ankle, a concussion, severe bruising, a…" She swallowed. "You might be afraid of trees for a while."

I tried to smile at her attempt at a joke. She was trying.

"We were all confused about the stitches," Lanna continued, lifting up my bandaged hand.

I'd all but forgotten about the slice below my thumb, since it was practically nothing compared to the rest of me. If I closed my eyes, I could see Seth's concentration as he tried to fix the damage he'd caused. I could almost feel his gentle touch. That was a terrible idea, and I shook my head to clear the memory. "I cut myself with a knife. Accidentally," I added as an afterthought. "It was too deep to ignore."

"So you stitched it yourself?"

Lying was easier than the truth.

"You poor thing," Lanna whispered.

I needed to think about something else. Desperately. "How did Matthew find me?" I asked. My mind was still fuzzy, but that didn't stop me from remembering how close I'd come to being back in Geller's hands. If he had managed to get me down the mountain, I wasn't sure what would have happened to me.

Smiling a little, Lanna returned to stroking the back of my hand. It was oddly soothing, and I wondered if she knew how much it helped keep me calm, just being touched like that. "My brother is nothing if not persistent," she said proudly. "I don't think he's slept since the gala, and it was killing him knowing he hadn't done his job."

"I wasn't his job," I argued. "He didn't have to look after me like he did."

"You're family," Lanna replied. "Of course he did."

Family. I didn't even know what family was supposed to feel like, but I guessed it was someone sitting by a hospital bed instead of getting much needed sleep. The last time I'd been in a hospital, Dad had simply sent an army of lawyers in to make sure no one in the press learned I was there for alcohol poisoning. At fourteen, I'd learned my lesson about ever expecting the man to care what happened to me as long as I didn't embarrass him.

"Matthew tried everything he could think of," Lanna continued. "I think he finally found a camera near enough to the gala to figure out which car you'd been taken in, and he followed it across the city using every gas station and ATM camera he could get access to. Once he figured out where you'd been taken, he found Officer Dunn."

Will Dunn, who had nearly gotten me killed alongside his friend because he valued his own life too much.

Lanna must have sensed my anger, but it confused her more than anything. "Dunn had been left for dead at the warehouse," she explained slowly. "He told Matthew where to find you and admitted Geller was on his way, since Geller had threatened to shoot down an entire restaurant if Dunn didn't cooperate. If Dunn hadn't told Matthew a shortcut, he never would have found you in time, and we're lucky Geller was more interested in finding you than making sure Dunn was dead before he left."

So I was wrong. About a lot of things. I didn't know how to acknowledge that, so I said nothing.

"He refused to get treatment until he knew you would be okay," Lanna said quietly. "He saved your life."

Guilt only made the hollow ache in my chest worse. "What happened to Geller?" I asked. Once I knew that, I could sleep. Sleep and hopefully wake up to the soft waves on a Bahama beach so I could discover all of this was a terrible dream.

"Matthew shot him," Lanna said. "Not fatally, but now he's in custody. Apparently he's part of some terrorist group, but I didn't really understand what they were telling Adam. He can probably explain it. But the important part is Geller can't get to you or anyone ever again. They won't set him free after some of the things he's done."

Like stabbing the only man who had managed to see the real Catherine Davenport. Killing someone I could have spent a lifetime getting to know.

"Catherine, what's wrong?"

"Seth," I whispered through my tears, though she didn't seem to understand. "Is he…? What happen…" I couldn't find the words. Did they go into the cabin and find him? Or was he still there, an empty shell of a man who didn't deserve to die like that? For me. Where was Seth's body?

Shaking her head, Lanna pressed her palm to my forehead and reached for something behind me. "You should sleep, Catherine," she said and stroked my hair, lulling me back into exhaustion as a wave of fuzziness brought me sinking into painless oblivion.

* * *

Never in my life would I have guessed being wheeled through the door of the Munroe Shack would bring an enormous sense of peace. Just seeing the little kitchen and the Christmas tree with its warm lights and the table where Matthew had beaten me at poker brought a strange smile to my face. And there was a small chance the warmth of it all filled in the hole in my heart, just a little.

It felt like I'd come home, and I'd never experienced that before.

"I know it's not great," Adam said as he pushed my wheelchair inside. "But we thought it would be easier for you to sleep on the couch down here instead of having to climb those stairs every day."

I could see Lanna's nerves as she followed us in, and I smiled at both of them. "It's perfect," I told them. "Really. Thank you."

"Of course it's perfect," Matthew said, joining our little party near the glittering tree and helping me switch from the wheelchair to the couch. "I finally get a bathroom to myself! Sucks for you two."

But Adam and Lanna just smiled as they stood there in each other's arms. They both looked completely exhausted—we all were—but somehow they still looked happy. Probably because they had each other. I'd never contemplated love—I was only eighteen, after all—but in that moment I desperately wanted to know what it felt like. Maybe making lasting connections that could deepen with time wasn't a bad idea after all.

"You guys should go to bed," Matthew continued. "I'll hang out with the cripple until she gets bored and pretends to fall asleep."

A week ago I would have hated him for that comment. Now I simply smiled and wondered how anyone in the world could not like Matthew Davenport. If I had been stuck in a cabin with him, I wouldn't have even noticed time passing just because his happiness was infectious. I had yet to figure out why my dad was convinced he was a miserable drunk.

"Cripple?" I asked as Matthew grabbed a blanket and tossed it over my legs.

He gently tucked the blanket around the cast keeping my foot immobile then settled on the end of the couch. "Sure," he said, though the lightness in his voice had settled a bit. "You managed to both break your ankle and half your ribs at the same time, which is not only impressive but absolutely gives you the distinction of being particularly inept at mobility."

"Big words," I muttered, but I couldn't keep up the happy mood either. It was almost as if I knew what he was going to say next.

"Catherine…" He sighed and leaned forward on his elbows, turning his blue eyes to me. Blue, but more gray than the eyes I'd grown used to over the last few days. "I'm so sorry," he said. "You tried to tell me, and I just… This was all my fault."

As his head sank low with his misery, I reached out and patted his arm. "You saved me," I said. "I owe everything to you."

He tried to smile when he looked up, but he wasn't very good at it. I must not have noticed before, but I had a feeling he wasn't used to smiling, even though I remembered him being a total goof when I was a kid. What had happened to him in the last thirteen years?

Taking a slow breath, Matthew scooted just a little closer to me and took my hand. "Will you tell me what happened?" he asked. "As much as you can remember? I need… I'd like to know. If you're up for it."

I'd already recounted my adventure more than I thought I could handle, speaking to the police—Will thankfully kept his distance, even if he wasn't to blame for what happened—and to the CIA and to Lanna and Adam. I'd even had to tell multiple doctors, just so they knew exactly how I'd gotten all my injuries. I had hoped, once I left the hospital none too soon, I wouldn't have to think about the last week ever again.

But considering he'd literally saved my life, Matthew deserved to know.

Starting with the gala, I told him about Giles acting weird—"He's in jail," Matthew confirmed when I told him the event planner was an accomplice—and I told him about seeing Geller and stupidly following him into the room. I told him about the other thieves, Will included, and about Geller's decision to use me for a ransom. Matthew told me they'd never gotten any calls, but likely it was because Geller had no idea I was staying with the Munroes.

"Good thing too," Matthew said. "Adam would have paid him in a heartbeat, and with what I've heard about Geller, he probably would have killed you anyway. We wouldn't have gotten you back."

Another tiny piece filled in the hole in my chest at the thought. I wasn't even Adam's family, not technically, but he treated me more like a sister than my own father had ever treated me like a daughter. Maybe, with my cousins' help, I'd survive this whole thing relatively intact.

When I told Matthew about Will's plan to set me free so I could escape to the cabin, he rolled his eyes. "I get the sentiment," he explained when I gave him a confused look, "but only an idiot would think he had no other option than to hide you away where no one could find you. Still, he likely saved your life with that move, I'll give him that."

"It took forever to get to the cabin," I continued, "but I finally got there only to realize Seth was already there."

Matthew held up his hand to stop me, his brow furrowed and his eyes harder than I thought they ever could be. "Wait," he said, the word almost a growl. "No one else has said anything about someone else being at the cabin."

Well that didn't make sense. "No one? I thought you talked to Will."

"I did," Matthew replied. "But he said nothing about you having company. Neither did Lanna, or the cops, or…"

Or me. I thought I'd said everything to the best of my memory. There was no way I could have left out something as big as Seth. "The CIA—"

"I talked to Agent Calloway," Matthew said, shaking his head. "She showed me her report, and none of us could figure out why Geller would take that much interest in you or work so hard to find where you were hiding when you have no connection to Homeland Security, which was his group's ultimate target. Who is Seth, Catherine? And why didn't you tell anyone about him?"

Was it actually possible to subconsciously omit every detail about someone?

Matthew jumped to his feet when I didn't respond. "What did he do to you, Catherine?" he asked, almost terrifying as he stood there. "Did he hurt you? Where is he?"

Tears pricked at my eyes, which only made things worse.

"Catherine, you have to talk to me. Tell me what he did."

"He died," I whispered and completely lost it, my tears spilling over and my breaths coming in sharp, agonizing bursts.

Matthew had no idea how to handle that response, and he stood there staring at me in utter bewilderment, probably trying to figure out what to do with the sudden lack of target for his misplaced anger. It felt like forever before he sat down again and stared at the gas fireplace as he muttered, "I'm sorry. I didn't mean…" Then he looked right at me, his gaze intense enough to stop my crying. "Tell me," he said. "Please."

So I did. I couldn't figure out how I managed to do it without sobbing over my lost friend, but I told him everything about Seth, from his wound to his nightmares to him rescuing me from the trees. I told him about the first time he attacked me in his sleep, and how he was the reason I didn't starve or burn the place down. I told him about how something shifted between us in those last moments. How Seth changed from an unfortunate complication into something comfortable. Welcome, even.

"He saved my life, Matthew," I finished softly. "He lost his own to save mine. And I can't repay him for that."

Matthew had stayed relatively quiet during my tale, offering only the occasional grunt or asking a small question or two. It was hard to tell what he was thinking, with his expression mainly thoughtful, but I wondered if maybe he would have some insight as to why I had so completely changed my mind about the soldier. He'd started as another enemy and ended as a dear friend who saw me for me when no one else had.

"Seth Hastings," Matthew said finally, and his eyebrows rose in appreciation for my taste in friends. "I wasn't anywhere near the Special Forces in my Army days, but even in my division Hastings was legend."

That didn't surprise me. I didn't exactly know him well, but what little I *did* know of Seth told me he didn't mess around with his job. Even if he wasn't always successful, he had risked his life more times than I could guess to do his duty and save lives. And he'd made that wager one too many times, it seemed. His luck was bound to run out someday.

"You said he was stabbed in Laos?" Matthew continued, his words still full of awe. I nodded, and he whistled low. "Even if he managed to get on a plane, it's hard to believe anyone could survive that long. Especially with an organization like Geller's hunting him down. Sorry, I don't mean to be disrespectful, but the man must have been a beast."

I found myself smiling. "It's okay," I said. "I'd rather remember him in a good way instead of the way I saw him last." Too weak to move, his blood spilling onto the floor, and his eyes thinking he'd failed me when he'd really won me just enough time to be found.

"But why didn't he just go to a hospital?" Matthew asked, though I didn't think he was really asking me. He'd turned his eyes back to the fireplace again as he sorted through this new information.

"Everything Seth does…" I corrected myself: "Everything Seth *did* was to help other people. I think he thought that by staying away from everyone, no one else could get hurt."

"Nobility can be pretty stupid sometimes," Matthew acknowledged, as if he had experience in the area.

"I just wish I knew how to thank him," I said, settling more comfortably on the couch as sleepiness started sinking in. So far I'd only slept with the help of medication, and I was a little worried about what I'd find on the other side if I wasn't completely unconscious. Dreams of Seth? Nightmares of Geller and his fellow terrorists? It was impossible to know, and I wasn't looking forward to any of it. But I was way too exhausted to stay awake much longer. "I just left him there," I continued, tears stinging my eyes. "Completely alone. He may be gone, but he's just… There's nothing I can do for him, Matthew, and I hate it."

Getting to his feet, Matthew bent and touched a gentle kiss to my forehead. "You should sleep, Kitty. You have a long road of healing ahead of you." Halfway through turning away to head upstairs, he paused, glancing back at me. "You know," he said, "if anyone knows about owing someone their life and being able to do nothing, it's Lanna. You should talk to her about Luke."

I fell asleep before I could really wonder what that meant.

* * *

It took me two days to work up enough courage to start a conversation with Lanna and ask her about Matthew's comment. I hadn't been avoiding her, exactly, but our minimal conversation since I left the hospital had been awkward and stilted at best. Neither of us knew how to act around the other, and I was pretty sure Lanna was afraid of bringing up anything that had to do with the last week. Still, when I asked early Christmas Eve if she wanted help making cookies, she practically fell apart with relief and happiness.

"Of course," she said, trying very hard not to look too excited. "Adam has *loved* these cookies ever since our favorite caterer introduced us to them, and I was so happy when Josh agreed to send me the recipe, since we're not at home this year. I just hope I'm making them right."

Getting around The Shack wasn't exactly easy, but I had quickly learned which pains were easier to handle than others. My ribs screamed at me anytime I tried to use crutches, but it wasn't like I could walk on my snapped ankle. So I hopped, and while the pain was ridiculously intense, at least I could still breathe by the time I settled on a stool opposite Lanna at the counter.

Lanna *did* look a little frazzled, her hair falling out of its braid over her shoulder and a dusting of flour covering the front of her apron. But she still smiled despite her obvious stress. I was starting to love that about her. No matter what she encountered, Lanna Munroe seemed to never take for granted the things that brought happiness into her life.

"What can I do?" I asked, resting my casted leg on the bench next to me and fighting a grimace as my entire chest caught fire with too deep a breath.

Lanna glanced at me. "You need to keep breathing deep," she reminded me. Apparently I hadn't hid my pain as well as I hoped. "Your dad would skin me alive if I sent you back with pneumonia."

A wave of pain spread through my chest that had nothing to do with my physical injuries. It felt like I'd only just arrived, and my time with my cousins was quickly coming to a close. It was only one day until Christmas. After the new year, I was back to a school I hated with 'friends' who didn't bother to make sure I was okay, even after someone leaked my story to an internet site so the whole world could know.

That was the first time I saw Adam Munroe angry, and when we discovered the site, I thought for sure he was going to explode as he retreated to the other room to use his influence to destroy anyone who was involved. I'd never liked him more than at that moment.

Lanna was still watching me, so I took as deep a breath as I could manage before the pain in my ribs became too much to handle. "I'm trying," I assured her. The last thing I wanted was to get sick enough to start coughing and make the hurt worse.

"Cookie cutter?" Lanna suggested with a smile, and she handed me the little metal outline of a Christmas tree.

As I cut cookies from the dough she rolled out and transferred them to a large tray, Lanna hummed lightly to herself. I almost didn't want to interrupt and just listen to her happiness, but I knew I wouldn't have the courage to bring up the things I needed to hear if I didn't suck it up and ask her.

I took a deep breath—*ow*—and quickly asked, "What happened to Luke?"

She froze halfway through pulling a tray of baked cookies from the oven, and for a moment I was afraid I'd overstepped. That was what I got for suddenly springing the question on her without warning. But it only took her a second to recover. Closing the oven door and setting the tray on the stove above, she turned back to me with question in her eyes.

"Matthew said something," I said with a shrug. "He said you knew about…owing someone. And not being able to… But only if you want to tell me. I don't want to make you uncomfortable."

With a little smile, she nodded and brushed her hands clean on her apron. "Luke," she said, and just saying his name brought a little twinkle to her eyes that I had only seen when Adam was around. "He was one of our gardeners. I was wondering when you were going to ask about him." Matthew had most definitely filled her and Adam in on the whole Seth situation, since I often caught the three of them talking in hushed tones, and naturally she had made the connection to how similar our situations were, just like her brother had.

"What happened?" I asked.

Grabbing a bowl of green frosting, Lanna joined me on the stools and handed me a knife so we could start frosting the cookies that had already cooled. "I fell in love with him," she said.

I was so surprised that I completely crushed the cookie I held. Crumbs falling all over my lap, I stared at her. "When was this?"

"Same time as Adam," she said. "I met both on the same day, in fact. Life was playing a cruel game with me, that's for sure, though I eventually figured out that the way I loved Luke wasn't the same as how I loved Adam. Still…" She nibbled at a cookie, but she only took the tiniest of bites, probably too distracted to notice what she was doing.

I couldn't stop myself from looking back at her with amazement. There was so much I didn't know about my cousin, and to think I had almost tried to run away and never look back. "How did your mom feel about all this?" I asked.

Lanna almost laughed. "She didn't know," she said. "Not until… If she had, I'm pretty sure Luke would have ended up being deported even though he was born and raised in California. Back then, she didn't see anyone who worked for us as anything more than servants."

I took a bite of cookie as well, completely fascinated. I hadn't seen Lanna's mother in years, but I remembered exactly how she'd treated anyone who wasn't on the same social standing as us. I might have even patterned some of my behavior off of her, since I certainly hadn't learned it from my own mom. Unlike everyone else I knew growing up, my mom was positively a saint, and I had never understood how she and my dad even ended up together when they were so completely unsuited for each other. It was like something had forced them together.

Given my dad's complete dislike of my entire existence, I had my suspicions.

"Something was happening with Adam's work," Lanna continued. Though I could tell the story wasn't an easy one to tell, she did it with a smile, for which I was grateful. I needed her positivity if I was going to get through all this. "There was a man who thought Adam's dad owed him money, and when he couldn't get to either of the Munroe men, he came after me. Grabbed me from my own backyard."

I froze, forcing down memories of experiencing the exact same thing. I relived that moment far too often in my dreams, and I didn't need it working itself into my thoughts while I was awake.

"But Luke came to my rescue," Lanna said, and a tear appeared in one eye, glistening at the corner even as she kept frosting cookies. "He fought off my attacker and set me free, but the man had a gun. I wasn't sure what happened at first, but Luke managed to shoot the other guy first. He came to make sure I was okay, but the kidnapper wasn't dead yet, and…" She blinked the tear away, and it landed on her shoulder. A second later she pulled down the collar of her shirt and showed me a scar very near where the tear had landed.

"The bullet went right through Luke and into me," she said with a frown. "I think, if he hadn't been standing in the way, I wouldn't have been so lucky."

"And Luke?" I asked, though I was pretty sure I knew the answer. I took Lanna's hand, and she gave mine a little squeeze of gratitude as she shook her head. "Lanna, I'm so sorry. That's…" There weren't even words to put to it. She'd watched the man she loved die right in front of her, and I hadn't even bothered to care about any part of her life. No wonder my friends didn't care if I lived or died. I wouldn't have been surprised if most of them hoped I never came back.

"He saved my life," Lanna said, "and I didn't even get to tell him thank you. Or goodbye."

I knew exactly how that felt, and it was eating me up inside. "How do you get through every day knowing that?" I asked, desperate for her answer.

"It's not easy," she replied, which was exactly what I expected her to say. "Sometimes I have to take it one day at a time. Luke saved people. It was just what he did, and if I had to guess, Seth was the same way. And that means something. So I try not to waste Luke's sacrifice, and I do my best to remember what I learned from him. He changed my life, and I can't let myself forget that, or else everything he did was pointless." She put on a smile and reached for another cookie to frost. "Luke would want me to find the beauty in the world around me. The positive things. So I do."

"But I don't know how to do that," I said, panic rising in my chest. "I didn't learn *anything* from Seth except that I'm a terrible cook."

"And?" Lanna pressed. Apparently she knew something I didn't.

"I figured out how to build a fire," I grumbled.

She just smiled.

"And that I'm not as good at chess as I thought," I said, softer this time. "And I don't have to do everything myself. And the world doesn't revolve around me, though I think I knew that already. Even if I ignored it," I added when Lanna raised an eyebrow at me. "And…" I swallowed a lump of emotion that crept up my throat. "Seth taught me that I didn't have to grow up so fast. Be something I'm not. He let me be me."

Lanna reached over and gave me a side hug, surprisingly avoiding adding to my pain even though she held me tight. "As long as we don't forget what they've given us, it's okay to be sad sometimes and happy sometimes. I don't think Seth would want you to be miserable for the rest of your life just because you fell in love with him too late."

I crumbled another cookie in my hand, adding a painful cough as I choked on what she said. "Love?" I gasped. "But I wasn't… I barely knew… I hated…"

Lanna's smile was more knowing than I liked, but I couldn't demand explanation because she glanced up and immediately brightened. "Ah," she said and rose to her feet. "The best thing that came out of it all was this."

Adam hit the bottom of the stairs looking both confused and pleased, and he swept Lanna into his arms with ease. "I was coming for that heavenly smell," he said softly, "but this is better." He bent down and engulfed her in a kiss deep enough that I had to look away, though I couldn't help but smile. So good things could come out of sorrow, even if they weren't what you expected. If I could just remember that when I dreamed about my last moments in the cabin, maybe I'd survive.

Lanna's phone broke her kiss with her husband, and she barely moved away from him as she answered it with a breathless, "Hello?" Almost immediately, though, she stood up straight and took a step back from Adam. "What do you mean, gone?" She listened for a moment, nodding as concern—no, it was something different—wrinkled her forehead. "Yeah, okay. Thanks. He'll be there right away. Bye."

Adam was just as confused as I was as he waited for her to explain, a fire burning in his eyes. I could only imagine what the gardener was like if he managed to compete with *that*.

Lanna whispered something to him, and he whispered back, and even when I leaned as close as I could without falling off my stool, I couldn't catch a single word of their hurried conversation. In the next moment, Adam kissed Lanna's cheek then moved straight for the front door, grabbing his coat and his keys on the way out.

"Where's he going?" I asked Lanna, my heart pounding in my chest. "Did something happen to Matthew?" My cousin had been spending a lot of time in town the last couple of days, and it'd been hours since I last saw him.

"What?" Lanna asked quickly, but then she registered my question. "Oh. No, Matthew's fine."

"Then what—"

"Adam just had to run into town for something."

"But it's Christmas Eve," I argued. Adam didn't seem the sort to just abandon his wife on a holiday like today.

Lanna's smile didn't exactly put me at ease, but she certainly tried as she returned to put another tray of cookies in the oven. "They'll be back in time," she said with a finality that told me she wouldn't answer any more questions, no matter what I asked. A week ago I never would have guessed it, but Lanna had backbone.

But no matter how calm she pretended to be, I had a feeling the next few hours were going to be anxious ones, so I took a deep breath and prepared myself for the bad news that seemed to follow me wherever I went.

CHAPTER TWELVE

Thank goodness Lanna had stopped pacing, though I wished I could have joined her in it. She'd moved to the chair by the fireplace and was sketching in a notebook, though from what I could see it was mainly just tense scribbles with no real purpose behind them. I'd retreated back to my couch so I could stretch out my legs, but I hated lying down with only soft Christmas songs to break the silence of the house. Snow had started to fall, and I worried another storm was coming to lock us in and keep the others out.

It was almost nine. Adam had been gone for hours, and Lanna had only gotten a text or two from him. While her nerves didn't seem to get any worse, they certainly hadn't gotten better, and I was already aching from my own tension as I waited for her to explain what was going on.

"Lanna," I tried again.

I received the same tight smile she'd given me the last several times. "Don't worry," she said, though her words did the opposite effect.

"But Matthew—"

"Is fine." Her pencil dug into the paper, and the tip snapped. Sighing, she tossed her endeavor aside and rubbed her hands over her face. "I'm sorry," she said, looking over at me. "I know you're curious."

"Worried," I corrected.

"You don't need to be. There's nothing wrong with Matthew. Or Adam."

"That's not as reassuring as you seem to think it is," I replied. I grabbed the mug of hot chocolate she'd given me a few minutes earlier and held it tightly with both hands, wishing the warmth would spread through the rest of me and ease the tension that made breathing almost impossible. At that point, I was convinced that not even the warmest fire or the hottest bath could make me feel any better.

"Just try to relax," Lanna said.

I will if you will, I silently replied. Outside of her pacing, the woman had barely moved for hours, sitting in her chair facing the doorway as she anxiously awaited her husband's return. *What does that feel like?* I wondered. Even when I had sort of dated people in the past, I had never watched the door or waited by the phone. The only person I might have considered waiting for like that was gone, and it would be a *long* wait. Forever, in fact.

We needed a distraction before both of us snapped from our tension.

But before I could think of something to start a conversation, the front door opened, and Lanna was on her feet before I could even turn my head to see who came through. Running straight into Adam's waiting embrace, all of her anxiety melted with just a touch of his hands, and a pang of jealousy shot through me. I was only eighteen, but I wasn't sure I could ever find something as perfect as what they had. Someone who could fix all my problems just by holding me.

Someone coughed behind Adam, and they broke apart just enough to grin through the doorway. I couldn't see who was out there, but my heart started to pound a little as I strained to see out into the darkness. "Would you two stop?" Matthew asked lightly. "You're making me blush."

I settled back against the cushions with a roll of my eyes. Of course it was Matthew. Who else would it be?

Adam stepped aside, bringing Lanna with him so Matthew could come through the door with a mountain of wrapped packages in his arms stacked so high he could hardly see over it.

"Did you buy up all of Tahoe?" I asked with a strained smile. Lanna may have relaxed, but I was far from content. There was something the three of them weren't telling me, and I didn't like their secrets. I had enough of those from my dad, who still hadn't bothered to answer any of the calls or emails my cousins had left him.

Handing off his pile of presents to Adam, Matthew grabbed a small one off the top and crouched down next to me. His grin was infectious and at least partially warmed me up because it looked more real than it had before. "This one's for you," he said, holding the little box out to me.

It felt like there was nothing inside, and I stared at it for a moment, trying to understand why he'd be looking at me the way he was, with snow in his dark hair and his cheeks rosy. "Christmas isn't until tomorrow," I reminded him.

"I know," he replied, "but I figured you'd want this one tonight. Oh!" He stood, looking moderately alarmed. "I forgot one outside. Why don't you open that while I go grab it," he said and slipped out the door again.

I looked at Lanna and Adam, hoping they had some sort of explanation for their brother, but they were far too busy gazing into each other's eyes to even notice. Though I thought about waiting until Matthew returned, curiosity got the better of me, and I slowly peeled away the red and green paper until it was just a plain cardboard box about the size of my palm. I slid my finger under the lid and lifted it open, and then I turned it over to let a little diamond earring fall into my palm.

My earring, which I'd left on a chess board in the cabin.

"What is this?" I whispered, my chest constricting painfully as memories of Seth's grin filled my head. If this was a Christmas present, I didn't like it. At all.

The door opened again with a fresh wave of cool wind and a few flakes of snow, and I turned to tell Matthew exactly what I thought of his gift. But then I froze.

"Hey, Cat," Seth said.

I couldn't move, couldn't breathe, and my heart threatened to pound out of my chest. I was hallucinating. Dreaming. But Adam and Lanna saw him too, and Matthew came in behind him and met my gaze with a gentle smile. He was real?

"Seth?" I gasped and slowly sat up, every movement causing me pain because I couldn't focus enough to avoid it.

Seth matched my every wince as he stood there with a thin jacket on his large shoulders and a dusting of snow in his hair. "I'm so sorry," he whispered as his turquoise eyes traveled over me and rested on the cast on my foot. "That's…that's probably my fault. I should have stopped you before you even—"

Without knowing how I did it, I leapt up and threw my arms around his neck. He grunted in discomfort but immediately wrapped me in his arms so tightly that instead of causing me pain, it felt like he was holding me together. Tears stung in my eyes, and I still couldn't bring myself to believe he was really there, even when he lifted me off my feet so I didn't have to balance on my good foot.

"How?" I whispered into his neck.

Seth's breath shuddered, and he held me even tighter. "It's a long story," he said.

"I have all night," I replied. "I thought you were dead, Seth."

Taking the few steps needed to get me back to the couch, he gently lowered me down and nodded. "I was," he said. "Technically. For three minutes. Until Jameson brought me back."

I looked at my family, hoping they could explain, but they were already halfway up the stairs. So I grabbed Seth's hand and pulled as hard as my ribs would allow until he sat next to me on the couch. "Explain," I ordered. "Before I stab you myself for torturing me like this."

Seth's smile was only a half smile, which only made my heart pound harder than it was before. "CSI," he said softly. "Sometime after you were gone, he came into the cabin to take some photos and instead found me. I missed when I shot at Geller, and I must have passed out trying to follow him when he went after you. Jameson found me on the floor, barely alive, and he said my heart stopped when he was trying to wake me up. He performed CPR until I revived, and he was about to radio for help, but I stopped him."

Anger shot through me, thankfully masking the pain in my chest as I glared at him. "Why?" I growled. "Why wouldn't you let him—"

"I didn't know what happened with Geller," Seth replied, shaking his head and grabbing my other hand before I could hit him. "Or if I could trust Jameson. The fewer people who knew about me, the fewer people who would be in danger."

"Geller's group is gone," I said, still furious. "Matthew got Geller and the guys he had here, and a photojournalist over in Laos had enough evidence to take the rest of them down. You would have been fine."

Seth actually smiled wider, though he still didn't look completely happy. "Well I know that *now*," he muttered. "But I couldn't risk anyone else getting hurt. I offered Jameson a large amount of money to help me get as far as I would last and find a small-town doctor to keep me alive enough to go after you."

My anger vanished in a second, leaving sympathetic anxiety in its wake. "You didn't know," I whispered, my eyes wide. "You didn't know I was okay."

He lifted both my hands to his lips and closed his eyes. "I kept praying Geller would be smart enough to keep you alive long enough for me to find you," he whispered. "If I was too late…"

I lifted one hand to his scruffy cheek, and he pressed his face deeper into my touch. I wasn't sure what I could say, all of my words stuck in my throat, and we sat there for a moment until Seth opened his eyes again and put his hand over mine.

"I was just about to head back to Laos, where I figured he would go, when your cousin found me in Carson City," he said. "I thought at first he was one of Geller's group, but Matthew Davenport is about as far from a terrorist as they come."

Looking at the stairs leading up to the second floor, I tried to understand. Matthew had been gone a lot, yes, but if a man like Max Geller couldn't even find Seth, how did a private bodyguard manage to do it?

Seth chuckled a little, the sound regaining my undivided attention. "That Mr. Munroe has a hell of a lot of power behind his name," he explained, reading my unspoken questions. "As soon as he started making phone calls and offering bribes, it didn't take long for my helpers to confess where I was."

"And now you're here," I whispered, still not completely sure if I could believe it.

Nodding, he reached up and tucked some of my hair behind my ear. His gaze was so intense that I thought I might melt, but I refused to look away even for a second. If I did, he could disappear. "Now I'm here," he repeated.

And suddenly I realized that my biggest pain from the whole thing could be gone. "You saved my life, Seth. How can I ever repay you for that?"

He smiled, but it was still that half smile that didn't seem altogether happy. "Technically," he replied, getting close enough that our noses brushed, "you saved mine first. And I don't mean just literally." My stomach clenched, and he seemed to realize my horror as he sat back and looked at me. He took a slow breath then explained, "Before you got to that cabin, I'd given up. I could have tried harder to get help, but I didn't see the point in fighting anymore. Not until… You reminded me why I should stay alive. You saved me, Cat."

My chest felt like it was on fire, but in the best possible way. All of my pain, all of my grief, all of my guilt and stress and fear—it was all gone. Now that I had Seth close enough to hold, everything would be okay.

He seemed to be thinking the same thing, his eyes on my hands as he lifted my fingers to his lips again. This was different from the way he'd held me at the cabin, as if now that we weren't in danger, he didn't have the same inhibitions he had had before. I shivered at his touch, and he leaned closer. "I don't…" He took a slow breath. "I know I'm older than you," he said.

"I've never acted my age," I replied. I knew where he was going with this, and I wasn't sure if I wanted him to go there. I had spent so many days thinking he was dead that I hadn't even considered what the future could hold.

"And I'm pretty messed up right now," he continued, kissing my knuckles again.

I smiled. "You and me both," I said. "Know any good therapists?"

"I don't want you to think you have to stay with…" He swallowed, as if his words were stuck in his throat. "With me. You deserve to live a good life, and I don't know if I…"

I reached up and ran my thumb along the scar on his cheek, wishing I knew what I was supposed to say. For the last few days I had been wishing I got more time with Seth, time to understand him and help him and be completely myself around him. And now that I had it… Seth was basically asking me if I even wanted to be with him, and I could see in his face how much he needed an answer to that silent question as he kept his gaze locked on mine. And it wasn't like I didn't want to be with him. I wanted nothing more than to spend the rest of my life getting to know this soldier who was so much softer than he looked. But right now…

"Seth," I said quietly, "I think we should be friends."

He froze, tensing beneath my hands as his breath hung in his lungs. "Friends," he repeated, and everything about him, from his stance to his expression, turned even harder. For a man who had only a moment ago been offering to let me find someone my own age, he was taking this harder than I expected.

But I had to stay strong. It was important. "Yes," I said. "We don't even know each other."

He tried to shift away, but I held him firm even though it sent fire through my ribs.

"Seth."

Pulling out of my grip, he stood and looked every bit the cold soldier I first saw him as. "I should go," he said roughly. "With Geller's group out of play, I need to report to—"

I rose to follow him and made it three or four steps before he realized I wasn't staying on the couch, and his eyes went wide.

"Cat, what the hell are you—"

"Seth, I don't want you to go." I grabbed his arms, and he held me steady as I balanced on my good foot and tried not to show my pain. "I *really* don't want you to go. Please." I held onto him tight and tried to figure out how I could make him understand, though he leaned away from my touch. He still looked so pale, and I wasn't helping. I needed to make it better before he decided I'd given up on us. Especially now that I worried he might give up on himself if he didn't have someone to keep reminding him how much the world needed him.

"You need to sit," Seth muttered and slowly guided me back to the couch. "Before you hurt yourself more," he added with a grumble. He resisted my tugs to get him to join me, but he probably realized my stubbornness was going to outweigh my pain and make me chase after him again if he left. So he settled on the couch next to me, looking completely tired. Of everything.

Taking an agonizing deep breath, I brushed the hair off his forehead so I could kiss it, and then I made sure he looked me in the eye so he couldn't misunderstand. "I'm eighteen, Seth," I said. "And I just went through a horrible thing. And you have no idea how badly I want to kiss you right now, but that's what the old Catherine would do. I need…" I wasn't doing a very good job, and he looked more confused than anything. "I need to figure out who I am before I lose myself in you like I know I will. But I need you with me so I can do it because you're the only one who puts up with my crap and says it like it is. You're the only one who really sees me. So I need you to be my friend. For now."

He shifted his head to the side, trying to read my face or find a lie or just plain torture me as I waited for him to answer. What would he even say? After everything he had already done for me, I had no right to ask something like this of him. If I were kind, I would let him get back to his own life and forget everything about our little cabin adventure. He had enough nightmares as it was, and I didn't want to be another one.

I just wasn't sure if I could actually do it without Seth. I meant what I said, and it was only because of him that I had realized I needed to change in the first place. My lungs ached from holding my breath, and it felt like I would fall into a thousand pieces if he told me no. While I knew I would survive, especially now that I knew he was alive and well, it would be a lot harder to want to go on if he wasn't there to give me his strength when I needed it.

And then quite suddenly Seth smiled, and the transformation on his face left me almost too stunned to realize that for the first time since I met him, he actually looked happy. It was like a cloud had lifted from over the top of him and things were sunny again. But did that mean he would stay and be my friend? I couldn't breathe until I knew for sure.

Seth pressed his lips to my forehead, still grinning. "You know," he said, "I always knew you were smarter than you let people realize."

I just stared at him, waiting. That wasn't an answer, though it was enough to keep my heart beating another few seconds.

Chuckling, Seth kissed my forehead again as if he couldn't help it. "Relax, Davenport," he said. "Of course I'll be your friend. I've gotten used to having you around, and while I'm on medical leave I'll need *someone* to order me around."

Relief swept through me, and for a moment I felt like I might collapse as my tension dissipated with my exhale. "You're so mean," I whispered as laughter brightened his eyes.

He tucked some hair behind my ear again. "And you're adorable when you're worried." His thumb rubbed out the crease between my eyebrows, and then he bent his head close.

Matching his grin, I pressed my hand against his mouth before he got close enough to kiss me. His moan nearly made me change my mind, and I laughed when I read his expression. "I know," I said, rolling my eyes. "The one time I say no, and it's the time I want it most. But I'm serious about this whole friends thing."

His lips still on my fingers, he sighed. "You're going to drive me crazy, Catherine Davenport," he said, the words coming from deep in his chest.

I just smiled, doing what I could to look every bit the princess I used to be. "You and the rest of the world," I said proudly, though I wasn't sure how long I could actually hold my ground with him looking at me like that.

"Okay, you've had enough alone time!" Matthew's voice carried down the stairs just before he came into view looking wary but immediately relieved when he saw that I'd stopped Seth's attempted kiss.

Seth didn't shift his gaze even a little, keeping his bright eyes locked on me. I, however, gave my cousin a smile. "Thank you," I told Matthew. "For everything. If not for you…"

Settling in a nearby armchair, Matthew shrugged but returned my smile. "We're family, Kitty. It's what I'm here for."

I saw Seth's question before he could ask it, and I glared at him. "Don't even think about calling me that," I warned him, loving the laugh he gave me as he entwined our fingers.

"Lanna has the guest room made up for you upstairs, Hastings," Matthew said, and I heard his warning as much as I saw it in his look.

And still Seth refused to look away from me, as if he was afraid that if he turned his gaze anywhere but my face, all of this would be a dream. I knew the feeling. "Thank you, sir," he said.

"And I sleep lightly."

"Matthew," I complained. "Don't threaten my friend."

But Matthew wasn't done. "I may not have your size, Hastings, but I'm scrappy."

Finally Seth turned to face my cousin, at the same time shifting so we sat hip to hip. Thankfully he didn't put his arm around me, or I wouldn't have been able to resist curling up in a ball next to him and disappearing into his embrace. "You don't have to worry, sir, though I have no doubt you could take me down pretty easily. I've heard about some of the jobs you've dealt with working with Munroe, not to mention your impressive Army career. People still mention Matthew Davenport."

Flattery. *Nice.* Grinning, I dropped my head onto Seth's shoulder as Matthew fought against a smile brought on by Seth's ego boost.

"Besides," Seth added and rubbed his thumb along the back of my hand. "She won't even let me kiss her, and there's no way I'm going up against Catherine Davenport. What she says goes, and we're going to be friends."

I could have kissed him for that comment alone. Luckily, Matthew kept me back as he said, "Oh. That's…that's really good of you, Hastings. You're…surprising."

"I'm going to try my hand at being young," I explained to Matthew, but then I frowned. My cousin looked absolutely exhausted, but despite his changing opinion of my soldier, he seemed determined to stay until Seth went to bed.

And a sudden thought of horror struck me. I doubted that just because he wasn't dying anymore Seth's nightmares were gone, and if one of my family heard his screams and went to try to wake him up, I could picture quite vividly how Seth might unconsciously react, and it wouldn't end well.

Leaning close so Matthew wouldn't hear, I whispered, "Are you still having nightmares? When you close your eyes, do you…?"

His smile faltered a little, but Seth did a good job of hiding it. "Who would have guessed the infamous Catherine Davenport had such a heart?" he replied and touched his lips to my temple. "I think… I think you make them better. When you're nearby. Helping me breathe. That last night in the cabin, after I brought you in from the hill, I… No matter how worried I was that you wouldn't wake up, that's the best I've slept in months. It was nice to feel needed. Not just used."

Holy cow, he knew how to make a girl blush, but that didn't necessarily solve the problem. Luckily, I was pretty sure I had a good solution that didn't involve Matthew witnessing Seth's PTSD just yet.

"Matthew," I said, turning back to my cousin as he quickly pretended he wasn't trying to overhear us. "I need him nearby. Please. I can't…" Wow, this was harder to say than I thought. "I can't sleep without dreaming about…everything." Seth's hand tightened around mine, but I kept my eyes on Matthew. "The only time I felt safe was when Seth was next to me. I need him, Matthew."

Matthew glanced between the pair of us, and he must have sensed how much we needed *each other* because he nodded and rose to his feet, giving Seth a look of compassion. Suddenly I wondered if Matthew ever had nightmares from *his* days at war. Would he ever find someone to help him if he did? "I get it," he said with a little smile. "I'll see you in the morning." He moved toward the stairs, but, pausing at the bottom, he gave us a smile then added, "Merry Christmas."

I was safe and sound back home with my family, feeling stronger and happier than I had been in a really long time. Seth was alive and well and in my arms, for now willing to stick around until I could figure out who I was. We both needed some serious therapy, but we could get through it together, which was more than I could have dreamed. The snow outside was absolutely beautiful, the fire was warm, and I had my whole life in front of me. What more could a girl want?

"Merry Christmas, Matthew."

CHAPTER THIRTEEN

I'd never slept so soundly in my life. With Seth's arms around me on the couch, I felt like nothing in the world could touch me, and morning came all too quickly, pulling me awake almost as soon as I closed my eyes to fall asleep. The sun streaming through the window and onto my face definitely wasn't helping, and I scowled at it, hoping it would slip away and turn back into night so I could just stay where I was forever.

A grumble behind me brought a smile to my face. "Make it go away," Seth said into my hair. Apparently he wasn't a morning person either.

I pushed myself a little deeper into his hold even though the pressure hurt my ribs. I would much rather stay where I was. "I can do a lot of things," I murmured, "but I can't command the sun."

"Try speaking Turkish at it," he replied, his voice gravelly.

"I told you I don't speak Turkish."

Tightening his hold, he snuggled just a little bit closer. "I'm pretty sure you're a secret genius," he said, "so it's only a matter of time."

I could feel him breathe every time I did, and I wondered if he'd been doing that all night. "Any bad dreams?" I asked him quietly.

"Not when you're around," he replied. "You?"

"Not even a little." And while I knew I couldn't stay there in his arms forever, I wished I could. With Seth holding onto me, nothing could touch me. It would take a lot to convince me I needed to get back to reality, where I couldn't be right where I was for the rest of time. I just— "Is that bacon?" I asked, lifting my head as the smell suddenly overwhelmed the rest of my senses.

Matthew burst into laughter on the other side of the kitchen counter as Lanna and Adam both worked quickly on making other things like pancakes and eggs. "I told you," he said to his sister. "I had a feeling she was a bacon lover."

"The only thing she knows how to make," Seth said, softly enough that only I could hear.

I threw my elbow into his gut, careful to hit his uninjured side. He grunted, the sound a mixture of laughter and pain. "Sorry," he said, though I knew he didn't mean it.

Sitting up with a little help from Seth, I smiled at my little family so full of happiness. If I had known this was what family was supposed to be like, I would have found a new one years ago. "Can I help?" I asked as they started bringing plates loaded with food over to the table.

"Matthew was right," Lanna said and grinned our way. "You really were a good influence on her, Seth."

I felt him sit up behind me, his hand resting against my waist and keeping me in his secure hold. "Thank you, ma'am," he said, "but all I did was let her save my life. She did all the growing on her own."

I met Lanna's knowing smile with one of my own. Without Seth, I never would have come out of the ordeal the way I had, and I'd lost count of the number of ways *he* saved *my* life. Like I'd told Matthew the night before, we needed each other to be better. To be whole. And I would cherish him for as long as I was lucky to have him.

"Can we eat?" Matthew asked loudly. "I'm starving."

"Wait," Lanna replied, suddenly pink. "I have a present I want Adam to open first." From her pocket she pulled out a little envelope and held it out to her husband.

Even Seth froze, all of us holding our breath as Adam's thick eyebrows pulled together in confusion. He took the envelope without a word and slowly slid his finger beneath the cover to open it. Lanna kept turning more and more red, and Matthew glanced over at me with wide eyes, as if confirming he had the same thoughts as me. What else could it be?

The black and white ultrasound photo slipped from Adam's fingers almost the same second he saw it, and in one swift movement he wrapped Lanna in his arms and closed his eyes tight against the tears of happiness that slipped onto his cheeks. "When?" he whispered.

It looked like Lanna could barely breathe in his hold, but that didn't stop her from hugging her husband just as tightly. "July 27th," she said. "I wanted him to be a surprise."

"Him?"

Lanna laughed. "I'm just guessing."

I looked away when Seth rubbed his thumb along mine. I hadn't even noticed I'd taken his hand, and when he reached up and brushed a tear from my cheek, I realized I'd started crying.

"Good tears?" Seth asked quietly, a little bit of concern wrinkling his forehead.

"Absolutely good tears," I replied. "She's going to have a baby!"

He grinned. "I worked that out for myself, actually."

"Shut up," I said and grinned at him, so overwhelmed with happiness that it felt like nothing could go wrong ever again. Seth grinned back at me, and he looked so alive that I barely recognized him. And before I could make a comment about how *good* he looked, in every way, movement caught my eye and I glanced over at Matthew, who had come around the table to stand in front of us.

"I can't believe I'm about to do this," he said, glancing between us, "but it's Christmas." And he held out his hand, from which dangled a bundle of leaves with little white berries. I had used it often enough as an excuse that I recognized the mistletoe immediately, and I laughed.

"Really?" I asked.

Matthew frowned a little. "Give the man a kiss before I change my mind, Kitty."

So I did, pulling Seth close and kissing him in a way I'd never kissed anyone before. It was gentle, and still, and a whole lot shorter than I wanted it to be, but it felt like we were both saying so much in that kiss. It was a promise to each other. To support each other and to always see the real person beneath the mask. I didn't know what would happen to us in the future, if we would stay friends or become something more. For now, I didn't care. I was just glad I had him by my side, alive and strong and happy.

When I pulled away, Seth tucked some hair behind my ear and smiled. "You, Miss Davenport, are going to be the death of me," he said and helped me up so I could go offer Lanna and Adam congratulations. If not for that ridiculously warm smile that stayed plastered to his face as he guided me into Lanna's outstretched arms, I might have thought he was serious.

"Don't worry," I told him as we sat down to dig into our food a moment later. "We have plenty of time for us to drive each other crazy."

"Yes we do," he said and took hold of my hand, telling me in that gesture that he wasn't going anywhere.

The End

EXCERPT FROM BITTERSWEET BREWS

I wasn't entirely sure what brought me back to the coffee shop the next morning, but I got in line at eight and fervently hoped it wouldn't get me a cup of boiling water thrown in my face. The young owner hadn't forbidden me from coming back, but I had no doubt she wouldn't be happy to see me.

Half a second after meeting my gaze, she groaned and threw her sharpie at me, which I caught before it hit me in the eye. Impressive aim. "Why?" she grumbled, shaking her head. "Haven't you done enough damage?"

I wasn't used to people not liking me right off the bat, especially when I wasn't using my bodyguard persona. But I supposed our first meeting, though it had lasted all of a few seconds, hadn't given her the best first impression, and the second had only made it worse. Third time the charm?

"I wanted to apologize," I said, handing her the marker back. I glanced behind me to make sure I wasn't holding up a line, and then I gave her a sheepish smile that only deepened her scowl. Huh. "I didn't realize I would make things worse yesterday." She didn't seem to be stressing over whatever payment she apparently owed, though. Either she exaggerated the consequences of me intervening, or the thugs hadn't come back yet. Either way, I wanted to try to make it better.

She folded her arms and, after making sure the skinny kid who was making the orders was fine, jerked her head for me to follow her to the corner of the store so no one could overhear us, I assumed. "I shouldn't have gotten mad at you," she admitted, though reluctantly. She wouldn't even look at me as she spoke. "Ares—the one who kicked your butt—makes me nervous, and I had to put that energy somewhere."

Though her commentary on the fight stung, I decided to ignore it. "Does he come here a lot?" I asked.

She was about to answer when she changed her mind, clamping her mouth shut. Her eyes strayed over to her employee and the few customers at the little tables around the lobby, and then she sighed. "I have to get back to work. You can go now."

Seriously? "Wait," I said as I followed her back to the counter.

"I have customers to serve and an espresso machine to fix," she replied brusquely. "I don't have time to deal with your weird sense of nobility. I don't know you. You don't know me. Go find some cat to pull out of a tree or something."

What was her problem? "I was just trying to help."

She turned so quickly that I nearly ran into her. Again. And she looked right into my eyes with a determination that almost made me smile. Almost. "Look," she said and poked her finger into my chest. "Like I said yesterday. I didn't ask for your help, and I don't want your help. So either you buy some coffee and a donut, or get out of my shop."

I hadn't had someone talk to me like that since my military days, and it weirdly felt good to be ordered around again. Even if she was a girl several years my junior. Adam was painfully polite, and Catherine hadn't told me what to do in years since Seth had broken her out of her selfish ways. Outside of my nephew telling me which toy car I could play with, I didn't have anyone giving me orders, and I practically craved it. "Yes ma'am," I said and grinned at her. She didn't like that, which only made me smile more. "How about a decaf? And a bear claw."

She stared at me for a second as if I'd said something completely ridiculous, and then she let out an over dramatic sigh and slipped around the counter. "4.25," she grumbled and held out her hand.

I pulled out a ten and handed it to her with a wink, knowing she would hate that almost as much as she apparently hated me. My teasing hadn't gotten a reaction like hers in years, since Lanna and Catherine had both learned that the easiest way to shut me up was to ignore me. I had to admit I kinda missed that annoyed look she gave me. "Keep the change," I said, and she rolled her eyes.

"Of course you'd say that," she said and turned to get my food.

I quickly found a seat in the far corner with a view of the door. If the well-named Ares came back acting like his namesake, the Greek god of war, I would be ready to show him the door. And this time I wouldn't let him win so easily.

The shop owner arrived just a moment after I sat down, and though she didn't look all too pleased that I was still there, she dropped the plate with my donut onto the table and poured me a cup of coffee. "Eat your heart out," she said before walking away.

"Hey!" I called, and though she froze, she didn't turn around. I asked my question anyway. "What's your name?"

She spun on her heel, with the coffee in her pot sloshing dangerously close to the spout as she did. "Why do you care?"

"Indie!" her employee shouted to her, waving her over.

I grinned as she grimaced. "Indie," I said, deciding the name fit her well. "What's it short for?"

Clenching her teeth, she debated not telling me but seemed to realize I would just keep asking. At least she was perceptive. "Indiana," she said with a sigh.

"Like the state?"

"Like the professor," she replied and hurried back behind the counter to help her coworker, a bit of pink spotting her cheeks.

I watched her for a few minutes, and though she never once looked over at me, I had a feeling she was very aware of me sitting there. Especially because her employee kept glancing up and accidentally making eye contact with me, and one of the muttered comments he gave to his boss looked an awful lot like, "Are you going to make him leave, or what?"

I dearly wished I could see her response, not just because a part of me wondered that very question. She no doubt had some great insult to offer me. I would stay out of her way as best I could, but I was determined to stick around in case Ares and his buddy came back to cause more trouble, especially considering I'd apparently made it worse.

However, when my coffee turned cold and my donut was long gone, I started to realize it could easily be a long day. Yesterday the goons had been there around four in the afternoon, and it wasn't even ten yet. I needed something else to do, something to occupy me until

I could actually be of some help to the contentious Miss Indiana. Luckily, I had a whole bunch of family members who had plenty to distract me.

Seth answered after only a couple of rings, though his greeting was drowned out by some impressive shouting in the background. "Hang on," he said, and I heard two doors close before the near bellowing disappeared. "Sorry about that, Matthew. Catherine's not too pleased with the movers."

"Does she have them quaking in their boots?" I asked. I could easily picture my little cousin taking a bunch of big burly men to task for putting a wrinkle in one of her sweaters.

"I'm pretty sure a couple of them are crying," Seth replied with a chuckle. "Catherine's a force to be reckoned with."

I settled against the back of my chair, grateful for his easy conversation and lighthearted nature despite his occupation. He was good for my cousin, even if I didn't always like how often he showed me my shortcomings. "I thought intimidation was your job."

"Trust me," he said, "she's so much worse. We'll be lucky if there's anyone left to actually get her stuff across the country. So what's up?"

"Any luck with Sanford?" His contacts had thus far come up short on finding the weasel who tried to double cross Adam, and if someone like Seth Hastings couldn't find him, I didn't have a whole lot of hope. But I really needed to hear something good, or the days were just going to get longer and longer. Until I found Sanford and locked him—and his cronies—away, I wouldn't be able to rest easy.

"The man's a ghost, Matt. For someone who could barely hold himself together, I'm amazed he's stayed so hidden. Either he's got someone bigger and badder helping him out, or the sniveling imp he showed you was a mask."

"I don't like either of those options," I said, frowning. "I hate knowing he's still out there."

"Me too, but we'll get him. Hey, I gotta go. Sounds like Catherine's threatening to move everything herself to show them how it's done. See you soon."

"Apollo, nice to see you as always." Indiana's carefully neutral voice broke me from my phone, and I turned to the door just as she stepped forward to greet a tall and overly groomed young man whose stance mirrored almost exactly the two from yesterday. Add to that the Greek mythology name, and I was pretty sure he was another of the thugs I was here to intercept. But I had to tread carefully, for Indiana's sake as well as mine.

"Boss wants the money," Apollo said. He didn't sound as gruff as his warmongering counterpart, but I had no doubt he had similar training and wouldn't go down easily. He'd also managed to come at a time when the shop was empty except for me, which had to be deliberate, though I didn't think he'd noticed me in my corner yet.

Though her employee had retreated to the back, Indiana held her ground surprisingly well. "You can tell your boss exactly what I told Ares yesterday. I don't have the money, but I'll pay it double next month. It's been a slow few weeks, and now Orion's gone and broken the espresso machine."

Apollo took a step closer to her. I rose to my feet, knocking my chair back a couple inches so it scraped against the linoleum. Both of them turned toward me.

"Don't," Indiana said, pointing at me.

But Apollo's attention was already firmly fixed my way. Just like Ares, he seemed to fit his name impressively well, a musical quality to his words and a boyishness in his face that probably belied his age. "You're the moron who got in the way yesterday," he said. It wasn't a question.

Moron? I raised an eyebrow, wondering if that was really the best word he could come up with for me. "I might be. I'm a friend of Indiana's."

She replied immediately: "He's not my friend."

I pretended to be insulted. "Ouch."

"Stay out of this," she snapped, adding a name under her breath that was a lot more like what I expected from her buddy Apollo.

Apollo, it seemed, wasn't as quick to action as his friends, and he stood calmly assessing the situation with a logical air about him. He knew from yesterday's encounter that I wasn't scared of the potential pain, and I'd obviously taken an interest in the young shop owner. Taking me in for a moment, he turned back to Indiana and muttered a quick, "We'll be back, Fierro," before slipping out onto the street.

Indiana Fierro. What a great name.

"You," she snarled, crossing the store so quickly that I actually took an instinctive step back in alarm. Two massive thugs, no problem, but apparently I had no bravery when it came to a five foot four woman in green Converse shoes. "You need to leave. Forever."

Something about her insistence really made me want to stay, and I couldn't help but smile as she tried very hard to look intimidating but came up short. Catherine was only a couple inches taller than this girl, but my cousin had years of experience manipulating the people around her and knew how to scare people off if necessary. Miss Fierro obviously spent most of her life appeasing the people around her, not fighting them.

"What if I buy another donut?" I asked.

Her jaw literally dropped. "You're insane."

"I like to call it eccentric."

"I really will call the police if you don't leave."

I folded my arms, thoroughly amused and almost desperate to keep tormenting her, if only to have a little bit of my life not completely inundated with real drama. "And tell them what?" I asked. "That you're refusing to sell a man a donut? I'm pretty sure the cops will take my side."

She narrowed her eyes. "Funny."

"I think so." Her face said more than any words could, and I laughed even as I moved for the door. "I'll leave," I assured her, "but only because you're out of bear claws. Not because you scare me." I might have added that last part for my own benefit.

As I stepped out onto the street, I found myself breathing a little easier. While I hadn't had to fight and prove I was better than yesterday, at least I had gotten rid of Indiana's harasser. All in all, the day wasn't a total loss. Yet. I could only hope no other Greek gods attempted to get money from a hole in the wall coffee shop until tomorrow when I could return and send them packing, though I worried there was only so much I could do. If all three of them came together…

Better not to think about how quickly things could go wrong. My biggest problem at the moment was finding something to do until tomorrow. As I was quickly starting to realize, being jobless sucked.

ABOUT THE AUTHOR

Dana LeCheminant has been telling stories since she was old enough to know what stories were. After spending most of her childhood reading everything she could get her hands on, she eventually realized she could write her own books too, and since then she always has plots brewing and characters clamoring to be next to have their stories told. A lover of all things outdoors, she finds inspiration while hiking the remote Utah backcountry and cruising down rivers. Until her endless imagination runs dry, she will always have another story to tell.

www.ingramcontent.com/pod-product-compliance
Lightning Source LLC
Chambersburg PA
CBHW060752210726
48292CB00014B/2790